BILLIE'S GHOST

BILLIE'S GHOST

CHAD HAUTMANN

A PLUME BOOK

PLUME
Published by the Penguin Group
Penguin Group (USA) Inc., 375 Hudson Street, New York, New York 10014, U.S.A.
Penguin Books Ltd, 80 Strand, London WC2R 0RL, England
Penguin Books Australia Ltd, 250 Camberwell Road,
Camberwell, Victoria 3124, Australia
Penguin Books Canada, Ltd, 10 Alcorn Avenue, Toronto, Ontario, Canada M4V 3B2
Penguin Books India (P) Ltd, 11 Community Centre,
Panchsheel Park, New Delhi – 110 017, India
Penguin Books (N.Z.) Ltd, cnr Airborne and Rosedale Roads,
Albany, Auckland 1310, New Zealand
Penguin Books (South Africa) (Pty) Ltd, 24 Sturdee Avenue, Rosebank,
Johannesburg 2196, South Africa

Penguin Books Ltd, Registered Offices: 80 Strand, London WC2R 0RL, England

Published by Plume, a member of Penguin Group (USA) Inc. Originally published in
2002 by VanMeter Publishing, a division of Uptrac, Inc., in paperback.

First Plume Printing, November 2004
10 9 8 7 6 5 4 3 2 1

Copyright © Chad Hautmann, 2002
All rights reserved

Page 165 represents an extension of this copyright page.

 REGISTERED TRADEMARK—MARCA REGISTRADA

CIP data is available.
ISBN 0-9673667-6-3
ISBN 0-452-28481-3

Printed in the United States of America

PUBLISHER'S NOTE
This is a work of fiction. Names, characters, places, and incidents either are the product
of the author's imagination or are used fictitiously, and any resemblance to actual persons,
living or dead, business establishments, events, or locales is entirely coincidental.

To Jeannie, for her unwavering faith and love and for the nights we shared by candlelight the roughest drafts of this book. And to Isabel and Sophie, for reminding me every day that love is boundless.

Acknowledgments

A number of people generously offered their time, knowledge, and support to help me with this book. First, a warm thank-you to my editors, Ryan Harbage and Julie Saltman, and my agent, Wendy Schmalz, all three the best, and surely the kindest, in the business. Thanks also to Trena Keating, Larry Myers, Richard Derus, Donna Price, Maggie Ball, Sharon Zuccaro, Ray McNally, Liz Heath, Hilary Winter, Jerry and Julie Kerr, Jim and Alexandra Gunderson, and Sally Steppling. I am lucky to know you all. And love, of course, to my mother, father, and sister, Lynn.

Was it a vision, or a waking dream? Fled is that music:—Do I wake or sleep?

—JOHN KEATS

CHAPTER 1

When I was five years old, an older cousin told me that if you swallowed while you were lying down, you would die. Not long afterward, a playmate revealed that if you fell asleep outdoors, ants would crawl in your ears and eat your brain. About that same time, JFK got it while I watched, and my view of the world was complete: it was a dangerous and arbitrary place, and you had to be ever vigilant to keep from stumbling into some gross humiliation, or worse.

All of which is to say that you would think I had been somewhat prepared for Virginia's death, but I was not. Virginia was my wife, and she was killed by a Winnebago driven by a dozing Canadian tourist. He, along with his wife and golden retriever, crossed the center line on State Road 951, the thin strip of highway that connects Naples and Marco Island. My wife, driving north in her Dodge, never even hit the brakes. Sometimes there are no breaks.

A friend of mine from college, now a lawyer, flew down from Atlanta to be with me. He helped with the arrangements and put his hand on my shoulder when I would suddenly begin to cry.

A few days after the funeral Richard said, "They shouldn't get away with this. They should pay for this." He had discovered that the Canadian tourist was a retired paper company president who had a winter home on the water on Marco Island.

"They'll settle out of court," he said. "I guarantee it."

So Richard, with me tagging along zombielike, met with the McNamaras and their lawyer in a plush office in downtown Naples. As I listened to him describe Virginia and our life together, I saw tears welling behind Mrs. McNamara's bifocals.

"Forget it," I said. "Just forget it. I'm tired. I want to go home."

I would not accept a reward for what I had done.

The McNamaras' lawyer jumped up, shook my hand, and smiled. Out in the parking lot Richard said, "You are a fool."

"I guess I am," I said.

Richard went back to Atlanta, and I returned to a house so full of memories that it leaked.

I had already lived longer than James Dean, Jimi Hendrix, Marilyn Monroe, and Bob Marley, not to mention Byron, Shelley, and Keats. That made me feel like something of an underachiever, and I suppose I was. I was the director of the remedial English lab at Edison Community College in Naples. Until I quit working. Until Gin's death. I was qualified to be a professor there and was repeatedly asked why I never applied for a position. After all, a professorship would've doubled my salary. It was simple, really. I had this problem talking to people when I didn't think they were listening, and some of my students didn't even pretend to care. But as I said, that was in the past. I got by on our savings and the small life insurance policy Virginia and I took out when we got married. Gin's parents held the mortgage on the house, and after the accident they did not once ask about payments, much less comment on how they were often late or nonexistent. I was not trying to be delinquent; sometimes I just forgot it was the beginning of a new month.

I was grateful for the house. It was my refuge, serving as protective custody and home. I shared it with one other creature, Mashed Potatoes, the puffy white Himalayan cat with flyaway hair that Gin brought to our marriage. I had never been much of a cat fancier, but now M. P. and I were almost inseparable.

The house was an old house—I liked to call it a bungalow—in an old part of a town that revered luxury over character. In other words, most worthy Neapolitans would have considered my place a dump.

It was hardly that. At times the house seemed almost organic, growing, ugly and irregular, out of the sandy soil. Orchid, mango, and palmetto palm trees, and a massive Cuban laurel, all untrimmed for years, kept direct sunlight from ever entering the rooms. In the half-light Mashed Potatoes and I would pass each other and nod, often going days without uttering a sound.

I was grateful, too, for the dense foliage. Shortly after Virginia's death I became completely nocturnal. I would awaken between 5 and 6 P.M., do what few household chores needed to be done to keep the place livable, feed Mashed Potatoes, and wait for dark. There was a beautiful silence and privacy to being awake when most of the world was asleep. There were no phone calls and no visitors. My friends had, for the most part, lost interest in me, as I'd let their repeated phone messages and letters go unanswered for months.

Late at night I would do my shopping at Naples' only 24-hour supermarket, and on those occasions I'd see no one but the bored and sleepy cashier. Well after midnight I'd go out by the darkened pool, followed closely by M. P., turn on the small rock fountain I repaired when we bought the place, and sit in a plastic chaise longue drinking beer, smoking my pipe, and listening to the trickling water. The hours would pass with the only interruption being an occasional light from next door as one of the Foster boys made his way to the bathroom. M. P., of course, loved this arrangement and would patrol the screen enclosure till dawn, rousting lizards.

Other nights I would sit in my wicker chair or lie on the living room floor and listen to jazz CDs. The classics, mainly. John Coltrane, Thelonious Monk, Ella Fitzgerald, Sarah Vaughan, Charlie Parker, Billie Holiday. Virginia and I had built up the usual eclectic music collection—old rock and roll, folk, reggae, some classical—but only the jazz worked like a great drug, not one that dulled pain and with it everything else, but one that revealed that, "This is the way it is. Take it or leave it, my friend." Miss Holiday seemed to know this better than anyone.

How many weeks and months this routine went on, I'm not sure; without my notice, a heavy funk had settled into the house like an unannounced relative. It stood quietly in the corners, a strange uncle with a lampshade on his head, unsettling and impossible to ignore. So be it. I would play out my time as the drunk hermit of the night. Anything else seemed irrelevant.

Then I got a roommate.

CHAPTER 2

To say that I lived in the past would be trite and not entirely accurate. Instead, I relived it. I was a memory artist, and I surrounded myself with my work. I washed the walls and furniture and knickknacks in scarlet, amber, and indigo, the colors of emotion. And, luckily for me, I got my inspiration from the simplest suggestions.

I'd see a pipe cleaner, twisted and discarded, and suddenly it was Valentine's Day, years ago. I took one, new and starch white, and bent it into the shape of a heart. Another, trickier, I shaped into an arrow and wrapped to pierce the heart. Nicely done, I thought, a fuzzy wire Valentine—and I placed it on the pillow where Gin was sleeping. Her eyes opened, her face scrunched, she reached for her glasses to see what it was. The smile.

"So you're telling me I can never quit smoking?" I said.

*   *   *

Or I'd stare at the bare blue bathroom wall until it became a stage, the opera. We squirmed in our seats, so much in love we had no patience for the couple who pretended onstage. Besides, he was too round and loud and old to proclaim himself to be a teen. Before intermission we slipped to the lobby. A quick stop at the men's and ladies' before home and bed. Silly, but the separation's

too long, so we invented a code for such times. I knocked—
Shave-and-a-haircut. . . Knuckles smarted on the solid wall. Then,
faintly, from across the way, her reply—*Two-bits.* A minute later,
wrapped together, we ran for the car, huffing with laughter at
nothing.

Ah, but memory is a most unreliable medium.

I read somewhere that the process of remembering triggers
chemical changes in the brain that alter the memory itself. So
what you remember is just a loose re-creation that grows less accurate with time. In short, what you think you recall never happened quite that way at all.

Yep, I was working in vanishing paint, but what else was there?

One night, about a year after the accident, I was out by the
pool as usual, lost in the sound of the fountain, when I thought I
heard, from inside the house, the single exclamation "Oh." Not an
exclamation of surprise or understanding or recognition. Just
"Oh." I did not hear it again and soon forgot about it, returning
to the mantra of the fountain and M. P.'s steady, silent prowl.

Several nights later, I lay on the living room floor, stereo and
lights off, thinking, again, or still (it was a loop that played nonstop in my brain), of Gin's accident, the moment of impact, what
she'd been thinking when lights suddenly blinked out, the terri-
ble scene, a funeral I couldn't recall, and then back to the beginning—Gin's white Dodge, intact, headed toward home. . . .

That's when I heard it again, this time longer—*"Oh Oh
Oh"*—a single note more held than repeated. I sat up and looked
at Mashed Potatoes curled in the wicker chair. One eye glowed
back at me.

"You heard that, too," I said, hoping. I put on Billie Holiday
and cranked it up loud. By the time I turned it off, after three
times through, the sky was getting light, so I went to bed.

The next night I waited. I turned off the fountain and sat by the pool in silence, listening. Nothing. Not an "Oh Oh," not a syllable. I got an idea and went inside. I pulled a step stool from the utility closet, climbed up on it, and pressed the test button on the smoke detector in the kitchen. The alarm split the silence like a scream. A light came on in the Foster house. Okay, so it hadn't been the alarm. I walked down the hallway—by now I had become quite adept at seeing in the dark—into the bedroom and began jiggling cords on the television and clock radio, searching for some loose connection that might make either come on spontaneously. I did the same with the radio in the spare bedroom. Satisfied that the sounds had been nothing more than the squirrelly product of too much time spent alone, I returned to the living room, sat down on the floor next to the wicker chair, and scratched Mashed Potatoes' belly.

"I think your daddy's going nuts," I said. She purred louder.

"Gin, I'm losing it."

"Ooh Ooh Ooh . . . what a little moonlight can do-oo . . ."

My spine froze. Unmistakably, it had come from my bedroom, a voice husky but definitely female. I went to the kitchen, felt for a knife in the drawer, and quietly inched my way down the hall. I could feel M. P.'s warm breath on the back of my ankle.

"Virginia?" I said, surprised at the tiny sound of my voice. I moved closer to the dark outline of the doorway.

"Virginia?" I said again. No response. "Gin?"

"Yes."

I swallowed a breath.

"What I mean to say is, I'd love some, honey. Are you buying?"

I hollered and stepped back. M. P. shot down the hallway, disappearing into the black of the living room. Silhouetted against the picture window near the bed was a woman, sturdily built and apparently dark complected. She seemed about my age, maybe younger, closer to thirty. She wore a dark dress, broad-shouldered, with sleeves that reached her elbows. In the moonlight that squeezed through the blinds, I could see what appeared to be a flower in her hair. An orchid from the tree out front.

I flicked on a small table lamp in the hallway.

"Who the hell are you?" I said.

"Eleanora," she said. "Pleased to make your acquaintance." Stoplight-red lips spread into an enormous smile as she moved toward me.

I gripped the knife tighter. "Hold it," I said.

"What are you planning on doing, honey? Separating me into sections?"

I looked down at my weapon, a grapefruit knife. My ears burned in embarrassment.

"What do you want? How did you get in here?"

"Through the door, doll," she said. "You left it open. Very dangerous." She smiled again and rolled her eyes suggestively. It had the effect of putting me a little more at ease. But still . . .

Suddenly, she rocked from side to side, raised her palms, looked toward the ceiling, closed her eyes, and sang:

"You get bold; you can't resist him,
And all you say, when you have kissed him, is
'Ooh Ooh. . . What a little moonlight can do. . . .'"

Her voice, slightly off-key, boomed through the house. Lights came on at the Soleweckis' next door.

"Jesus Christ," I said. "I've got neighbors. What the hell are you doing in here?"

"Honey," she said, her lips thick and moist, "this would be a much pleasanter discussion if we were sitting down. And I think you offered me a drink."

With Eleanora seated at the table in the Florida room (I kept a peripheral eye on her), I reached for two glasses from the liquor

cabinet but hesitated before sliding open the glass. Virginia had always kept the cabinet stocked for when we entertained her
clients, and I realized that I had touched nothing inside since her
death. Now I looked at her neat arrangement of cocktail glasses
and wineglasses, rims down on white linen towels, next to them
the bottles, grouped by liquor and brand, labels carefully turned
out.

"Sweetheart," Eleanora said, giving me a start, "size doesn't
matter. Any old glass will do."

Reluctantly, I removed two and a bottle of Jim Beam. I
poured, and before I could say, "Would you like some Sprite or
ice with that?" Eleanora had tossed hers back, emptying the glass.
Her eyes closed and she made a gentle purring sound.

"Don't know the last time I had a drink that tasted so good."

I poured her another, set the bottle on the table, and sat down.

"You've got some explaining to do," I said.

"You have any smokes?" she said.

CHAPTER 3

Her story was as strange as her sudden appearance in my bedroom. She was a singer, she said, though she had not worked in a while. She had last worked clubs in New York, and, since there now seemed to be little demand for her there, her manager had sent her south—way south.

"But why, for God's sake, *Naples?*" I said. "Why not Miami or Tampa?" I sipped my drink and winced at its sharp slide down my throat.

She said, "I never question my manager. He's the man, my daddy, and he never steers me wrong."

On showing up in my bedroom at three-thirty in the morning, she said that she had heard there was a room available on Twelfth Avenue. That much was true: Mrs. Turnbull, several doors down, was always taking in boarders. Being a night person, Eleanora said, she found this the only reasonable time to visit. The smoke alarm I'd set off had caught her attention, and, unsure of the address of the rental, she had tried my door and found it open. Lost in the dark, she had wandered back to my bedroom.

It was a hard story to swallow. But, and I don't know why, I enjoyed her company and had already spoken more words to another human being than I had in several months. I poured us both another glass of whiskey, resisting the urge to dilute mine with something.

By now M. P. had emerged from under the sofa, stopped in the doorway to look Eleanora over, presented a Halloween-cat arched-back pose, and dashed to the other end of the house.

"How about it, lover?" Eleanora said. "Do you have a room?" Her large brown eyes were moist from the drinks, her voice thick and low, sultry.

I surprised myself by saying, "You can stay in the spare bedroom tonight. You won't find any place else at this hour. We can talk about it when you get up. Where are your bags?"

"I travel light," she said, smiling. "And I thank you for the drink." She rose smoothly from the table—I half expected a stagger—and watched intently as I capped the bottle of Jim Beam. I returned it to the liquor cabinet, making sure that it fit perfectly into the ring it had left there and that the label was facing out.

I awoke after noon the next day with a headache, a raspy throat, and the fear that I had done something incredibly stupid. I could open the bedroom door to find the house robbed. After I fell asleep she could have let in others; she could be the point woman for a gang of gypsies. The house could be gutted for all I knew. Hell, when you got right down to it, I was lucky *I* wasn't.

Still, a roommate might not be such a bad idea. It would take some adjustments, sure, but I could set the rules from the start (no moving any of Virginia's things, for example). We both lived at night, which worked out well, and with her help, maybe I could make the mortgage payments on time. Her presence might take some explaining, especially to Gin's parents, but I would make it clear it was a roommate situation, that's all. If people couldn't understand that, well, tough.

Then again, I knew almost nothing about her, not even her last name.

"Gin," I said, quietly enough so someone in the next room would not hear, "what do you think?"

As I had been dozens of times in the past year, I was met with crushing silence.

I put on some shorts and an FSU T-shirt and padded barefoot to the closed door of the guest room. I listened for sounds of movement. There weren't any. I tapped lightly with just a fingertip. Still nothing.

"Eleanora," I said, barely above a whisper. Sounds of clinking metal and the soft thud of something hitting the floor.

"Eleanora," I said, louder. There was scratching on the other side of the door. I opened it a crack and out strode Mashed Potatoes, indignantly marching to her litter box.

"M. P., why are you bothering . . . ?" I looked up. The bed was made, the room empty, with no signs that anyone had spent more than a few minutes there.

"What the hell?" I said, beginning to worry. I quickly inspected the rest of the house and found it just as I, or we, had left it earlier that morning.

Perhaps she had reconsidered. Or maybe—and this was the frightening possibility—I had gone certifiably nuts. Insane. A case study. A full hour on the talk shows. If so, I thought, looking at the cocktail glasses in the sink, I was now drinking for two.

I spent the rest of the afternoon straightening up the house for Eleanora's possible return. Until I began, I hadn't realized how much I had let the place go. Virginia had always done most of the household cleaning, and by now the mess in the bungalow had become impossible to ignore. Newspapers, most never opened, stood stacked almost to eye level against the wall. Baseball-size tumbleweeds of dust and cat fur hugged the baseboards in most rooms and gently swayed each time I walked by.

In the den I opened the blinds for the first time in months, and the slanted rays of light revealed a universe of swirling particles. At my feet, Mashed Potatoes whined, undoubtedly curious about this sudden burst of activity and happy, it seemed, that the uninvited visitor was gone. I bent down and snatched her up, and that familiar rumbling began deep inside her.

"If I could put a handle on you and spray you with Endust," I said, "we could get this place presentable in no time." Her eyes closed in contentment.

CHAPTER 4

I had not always been a jazz devotee. Gin turned me on to the music, and at first I was a reluctant student. Jazz was the music of our parents, and I was familiar only with its modern mutant child: *smooth* jazz, *cool* jazz, *light* jazz, *soft* jazz, whatever the program director chose to call it, that seamless, soulless Pabulum that had glommed on to stereo dials all over the country. *These are the relaxing sounds of . . . ,"* the pudding-voiced announcer would always begin.

Jazz? No way. I love you, Gin, honey, but you can have that all to yourself.

She soon taught me differently. We began with the basics, in no particular order. We were improvising. Sunday afternoons, while neighbors mowed lawns and backwashed swimming pool filters, Gin and I sat cross-legged on the living room rug while she popped in CD after CD, and we ate mangoes from the tree out back and sipped coffee and tea.

We'd listen as Lionel Hampton worked raw-edged blues into subtle but deep emotion. There was Charlie Parker's rendition of "How High the Moon," with sax work that seemed to make vocals irrelevant, a useless appendage. Until you heard the heartrending irony in Johnny Hartman's voice, which, when accompanied by Coltrane on sax, McCoy Turner on piano, Jimmy Garrison on bass, and Elvin Jones on drums, created some of the greatest jazz—hell, some of the greatest music—ever recorded.

And the other terrific vocalists—Dinah Washington, Sarah Vaughan, Billie Holiday. Especially Holiday. This woman had lived, you could tell it, and each song exposed another nerve ending in her and whoever else cared to listen.

Through those early lessons, Gin said nothing. To explain would've been to destroy. It didn't take me long to realize that this was not the relaxing sound of anything. Quiet is not always calm; introspection is not relaxation. Or, as my recent visitor might say, "Relax too much, an' you're dead, lover."

Dead lover, the inescapable reality. Even good jazz couldn't for a second bring her back. I knew because I'd tried.

Virginia and I were lovers first, then we became pals. People sometimes remarked that we looked more like brother and sister than husband and wife, a comment that bothered me at first.

But now I know that when you connect with someone—really connect—a melding of minds, mannerisms, expressions seems almost inevitable, even enviable and sublime.

Gin and I would lie in bed at night, silent and unmoving, but both of us awake. (I had picked up from her occasional insomnia.) Then I'd sit up, and she'd sit up, and I'd say, "Fancy a walk?" and she'd say, "Help me find my shorts."

We'd walk the quiet streets toward Jungle Larry's Caribbean Gardens, a strange zoo/botanical garden hybrid, Naples' oldest tourist attraction. Gin would slip through a gap between the gate and a fence post, I'd go over the top and land in a sprawl, then we'd follow the crooked path past pens and cages and say hello to all the animals. We had to be quiet, of course, because keepers lived on the grounds, so we memorized the rocks and exposed roots that dotted the way.

On full-moon nights the place was downright spooky, the shadows of gumbo-limbo, sausage, and banyan trees playing delightfully with our minds.

"The mandrill seems depressed," I said one night as we stared into his cage. He sat very near us, clutching the bars like Papillon. His blue nose glowed in the moonlight, and his languid eyes pierced the soul.

"We will write a letter to Jungle Larry explaining the situation," Gin said.

"There is no Jungle Larry," I said.

"I know that, but we will write the letter nevertheless."

We did, as soon as we got home, and the following season, the last time we sneaked into the park, we whispered congrats to each other next to the mandrill's new facility, complete with tire swings, ropes, and perches. The baboon, clutching the bars, stared out at us. His blue nose glowed in the moonlight, and his eyes still pierced the soul.

"Maybe we could take him home with us and let him live out by the pool," I said.

"Perhaps," Gin said. "We'll write another letter. And if that doesn't work, next time we'll bust him out."

I smiled. Gin squeezed my hand and kissed my knuckles, and we sat on a bench until the sun came up. Then we mixed in with the paying customers.

Eleanora did not return that night. Or the next. By the third day I had put the episode away as some sort of hallucination, not a dream or a nightmare, exactly, just a brief mental rupture brought on by isolation and a recent fondness for jazz. It was surprising how little this explanation troubled me. I did, however, learn one lesson from the strange visitor: make sure the doors are locked at night. It might forestall madness.

In less than a week I had resumed my old routine. I would wake up about the same time the schoolkids in the neighborhood got home, fix something to eat for M. P. and myself, add that morning's *Daily News* to the newspaper pile, then retreat, after dark, to the chaise longue by the pool to drink a few beers, smoke my pipe, and listen to jazz or the bubbling fountain till the mockingbirds would serenade me off to bed just before dawn.

One night, sluggish from the warm air and telling Gin about the day, I began to doze in the chaise and awoke abruptly with the feeling I was not alone. I closed my eyes again to make it go away.

"Hey there baby make up your mind,
'Cause I been waitin' such a long long time . . ."

I sat bolt upright. "Dammit."

There stood Eleanora, a few feet away. She threw her head back, lifted her palms, and belted out,

"Now baby or never,
I been so sad an' blue . . ."

Her voice quavered; she giggled. The obligatory light from the Soleweckis' bedroom flashed on.

"I'm a little out of practice," she said.

"What is it with you?" I said, my voice trembling. This was clearly too much. "I never gave you permission to come and go here."

"That's what I came by for, lover," she said. "Permission. I wanted to give you time to think about me. Did you miss me?" She smiled that damned devilish smile.

"Knock it off," I said. "If you think you're going to use me and this place for whatever it is you're doing all day and all night, well, you can just forget it."

Suddenly, I felt very silly standing there flailing my arms and raising my voice, and I knew the Soleweckis were getting an earful at their kitchen window. I walked over and sat down in a plastic chair. Eleanora followed quietly and sat in another, facing me.

"What is your deal?" I said, leaning forward. "Is it drugs? It's drugs, isn't it?"

"And what is your excuse, then?" she said.

I felt myself flush.

"I told you," she said, "I'm a singer. Jazz. Scat. I'm not a liar."

"Okay, I'm sorry. But you nearly gave me a heart attack. I can't stand this passion you seem to have for scaring the crap out of me."

"And I apologize for that," she said. "I just love to sing and sometimes can't quite help myself." She winked and reached over and clasped both my hands in hers.

"Do you still want the room?" I said.

"Yes."

"Will you keep some sort of regular schedule?"

"I'll try."

"Will you quit scaring the pants off me?"

"Hmmm," she said, leaning back and eyeing me. "Those pants *would* look nice over the back of a chair."

"You do a pretty fair Billie Holiday," I said, fibbing only slightly, a good fib. My back to Eleanora, I was testing her, probing, as I carefully removed from the cabinet the two glasses we had used last time we shared a drink. Uncanny didn't begin to describe the physical resemblance, but that could be accomplished with the right hairstyle and makeup. I turned in time to see M. P. creeping toward Eleanora, eyes wide, nose twitching. The two locked gazes, then M. P. wound herself around Eleanora's ankles and curled up on her black leather shoes. Eleanora smiled and lit an unfiltered Pall Mall. She had found her smokes.

"M. P. seems to like you," I said. "It's short for Mashed Potatoes. She's usually frightened by strangers."

"Then you two must be good company. Now let's see, I know your cat's name, you know my name. What do most people call you, doll?"

I had just set the drinks on the table and was about to sit down.

"I'm sorry," I said, leaning across the table, my hand outstretched. "I'm Casey. Casey Cooper. My folks overestimated alliteration." Her handshake was firm, almost manly. Nothing like the end-of-the-fingertips nonsense that some women offered. "And you're Eleanora *who?*"

"I'm just Eleanora. Simply Eleanora." She smiled and looked into her Jim Beam, twisting the glass to catch the light.

"Of course." I nodded knowingly. "It's a stage thing. Like Madonna or Cher."

She set down her glass, threw back her head, and roared with laughter, startling me.

"Oh, honey. I am no Madonna, not on my very best day. I got myself disqualified a long time ago. In fact, because I *liked* to *share.*"

"No, I meant . . ." I let it pass.

How to describe her voice? I had never heard another quite like it. It had the warmth and exuberance of an alcohol buzz without the slur. It was deep and did not so much emanate from her as rumble out. When she spoke, though her lips moved, I got the strange impression that the voice came not from her mouth but from somewhere deep in her chest. It was a bit unsettling, once you got it in your mind. One thing was quite clear, though. She did not like to use that odd voice, that strangely thrilling voice, to reveal much about herself.

Still, the conversation was pleasant enough. She talked a little about the cities she had worked in—Chicago, Detroit, St. Louis, even Miami—"so long ago, lover, it seems like a dream."

I told her about Virginia, how I had not gotten back on track yet.

"I thought that seemed unusual, man sleeping out by a swimming pool every night," she said.

I shrugged. What could I say? I wasn't about to tell a stranger what was wrong with me.

I set down my glass—I'd had enough—and rose from the table. It was well past my bedtime, with the sunrise squinting through the cracks just over Eleanora's shoulder. She stood up, too, and moved around the table.

"Thanks so much," she said, hugging me tightly. My spine stiffened. "You are a lifesaver."

I awoke after noon. The sun was brilliant and grackles squawked in the front yard, deviling a neighbor's cat. I got out of bed and headed down the hall toward the kitchen. I stopped abruptly, realizing I was stark naked, and hurried back to my room, glancing over my shoulder. This would take some getting used to. I grabbed a pair of boxers from a drawer and a robe from the back of the bathroom door. It had hung so long unused, it smelled strongly of mildew, making me sneeze repeatedly.

In the kitchen I found Eleanora, bent over and staring at the trickle of coffee from the coffeemaker as it filled the carafe.

"Good morning," I said. She jumped. "Shoe's on the other foot now, isn't it?" I said, smiling.

"I didn't touch it," she said, motioning at the coffeemaker. "It just went off."

"Well, yeah. I set the timer last night." I pulled two mugs from the cabinet overhead.

"Allow me, honey," she said, removing the pot. Coffee poured onto the warmer and hissed and spat.

"Eleanora, no," I said. "You have to wait till it stops." I pushed the pot awkwardly back in place. More coffee sloshed out onto the counter and my hand.

"Ow. Damn."

Eleanora looked at the floor sheepishly. "I'm sorry, doll," she said.

"You must drink instant," I said. There was an uncomfortable silence, and I wanted her to feel at home. "Listen, if you need to do some laundry or anything, I'll show you where everything is."

She sniffed at the armpit of her dress. "Do you think I need to?"

"Oh no, no. Not at all. I just noticed that every time I've seen you, you've been wearing that navy blue dress." I was pretty rusty on the small talk.

"Don't you like it?" she said.

"Very much. Yes, it's beautiful. Quite nice."

I scraped at a speck on my coffee mug, and Eleanora played with her sleeve.

"I suppose I could use some new clothes," she said, brightening. "I haven't been shopping in ages." She put a hand behind her head and did a Mae West shimmy. "The finest stores, I presume, are downtown."

"I'll get dressed and I'll take you," I said. I was caught up in her enthusiasm. "I'll show you where Gin used to shop. The mall is just . . ."

But the gleam had left her eyes. "I don't think that's such a fine idea," she said.

Puzzled, I poured us both a cup of coffee. "The mall is your best bet," I said. "There really isn't any shopping downtown. Hasn't been for years. Parking, you know." I sipped my coffee.

"I meant going with you."

"Nonsense," I said. "I don't mind. I've got nothing else to do. You're new here; you'll need some help finding your way around."

Her look was beyond skepticism. She eyed me as if I were deranged. I shrugged it off.

"Just let me pull on some clothes," I said, gulping coffee and placing the empty cup in the sink. "Back in a minute."

As I left the kitchen, I thought I heard Eleanora say something, but barely above a whisper. I thought I heard her say, "It's your funeral, honey."

What a curious thing to say.

CHAPTER 5

Eleanora also had an unusual reaction to my car. She was smitten with it. With a lewd grin she said I must have to brush the girls away like flies. I told her she was overdoing it. It was a seven-year-old Camaro, for Chrissakes, in a town where people in Bentleys double-parked at the 7-Eleven. Still, she seemed to perch in her seat and clutch the door handle as if she were in a Formula One race car. Her nervousness increased when I insisted she wear her seat belt, which I had to pull and buckle for her. When we got to the mall a few minutes later, her agitation only grew worse. I got out of the car, locked and closed the door, but Eleanora stayed put. I dug the keys back out of my pocket and popped open my door.

"Can't you get the belt off?" I said, leaning in. "That one can be a little tricky." I reached across, hit the release, and the belt recoiled behind her.

"I'm going to wait here a minute. You go on in, doll," she said.

"Why? Is something wrong? Do you feel okay?"

"I'm just fine, and I'll be along as soon as you get going. Go. Go." She waved me away dismissively.

I closed the door hard. Hell, I didn't need this. I was just doing the woman a favor. I hated the mall. This was why I never went out. People were too damned weird.

I did not look back until I got to the door of Burdine's. Eleanora was just emerging from the car. She waved me on again, to go through the doors. I did but waited just inside.

"Are you embarrassed to be seen with me?" I said as Eleanora stepped cautiously inside. She turned abruptly and walked over to a display of bath towels. She began to inspect them, one at a time, turning them over, checking labels. I followed her.

"What is it? Did I do something to make you mad?"

"Honey, I'm not dragging you," she said, still not looking up. "But you have to live in this town. I don't want to cause trouble for you, that's all."

I told her I did not understand.

"For one thing," she said, moving on to fancy kitchen towels, "you're barely dressed." (I wore blue-jean shorts, a T-shirt, cross-trainers, no socks.) "And, in case you hadn't noticed, we look like salt and pepper."

So her manager had, apparently, told her a little something about this place. Naples was primarily a retirement community. It was aswarm with well-off old people from the stolid Midwest, the paradise they had worked their entire lives to realize. They wanted to keep it that way. To many of them, homogeneity was a virtue, difference and dissent a threat. The local paper often ran letters to the editor denouncing queers, sinners, liberals, welfare cheats, hobos, and the socialists who ran the country. The police were kept hopping with complaint calls about foraging ducks and kids running amok on the beach. It was sometimes a difficult place to live.

But give a black woman and a white man trouble for being together? Unlikely.

"You're being ridiculous," I said to Eleanora, and for emphasis I gave her a peck on the cheek. She looked at me, shocked.

"I didn't mean anything by that," I said quickly, backing up a step. "I was just making a point."

"You made it," she said, rubbing her cheek. I felt myself redden.

Eleanora sought out Women's Apparel like a bloodhound. I did my best to keep up, weaving through the racks of clothing that were always placed too close together. Finally, Eleanora slowed. A terminally bored salesclerk, likely a high school student, asked Eleanora if she needed help. She gave Eleanora a head-to-toe perusal with the condescension only a teenager can muster.

"I need some new rags," she said. "Dresses mainly. Something lightweight and hep."

I smiled; the clerk rolled her eyes.

"Okeydoke," she said, her enthusiasm as transparent as glass. "Let's see, you look like a size twelve."

"Eight," Eleanora shot back, and I decided I wanted no more of this. I told her I was going to hang around someplace else and that if she needed me, to holler.

I looked around for a chair but ended up sitting on the stand of a mannequin wearing half a bikini. This was my first trip to this store, or the mall, since Gin had died, and I could not help but think of all the hours I had spent just like this, bored stupid, waiting for Gin to just "peek at a few things." It had been a colossal waste of time that I would give everything I own to relive.

I did not notice Eleanora till she spoke.

"Whadya think, doll?" she said with a huge grin.

I don't quite know how to describe what she was wearing, mainly because I don't know what it would be called. It was a dress, to be sure, almost knee-length, quite puffy below the waist. The top part was black and shiny, her breasts straining the seams, the bottom white with turquoise stripes. It was a cross between a freshman's prom dress and a Carmen Miranda outfit. The clerk had dressed her as a clown.

"Do *you* like it?" I said.

"I don't know if it's me," she said, positioning herself in front of a mirror. She turned, examining the back, fluffing the ruffles. "But if it'll help me get a gig here . . ."

"I think someone is having fun with you," I said.

Eleanora looked puzzled.

I tried to make a joke of the whole thing. "Ain't nobody'd wear that," I said.

Her face turned sour. "You mean that little girl dressed me up like this for laughs?" She clenched her fists. "That was a low-down thing to do. I'll show that pimple-faced little tart who she's monkeying around with."

I jumped up to intercept her as she started for the salesclerk. She was hard to slow, and I had to dig in my heels to bring her to a stop.

"Let it go, Eleanora."

"She tried to drag me. She don't even know me." She had fire in her eyes. I feared a full-blown scene.

"She's a kid," I said. "She's just full of herself. You said you didn't want to cause trouble for me. Well, you're about to."

She relaxed enough that I felt safe letting her go. As I did, she bolted.

"Eleanora, don't."

"I'll find my own damn clothes," she said, pushing through racks and rattling hangers. "Don't need no little bitch dressing me." And she began peeling off the abominable garment as she walked. I turned and pressed on my eyelids. I felt a wicked headache coming on.

★   ★   ★

I waited twenty minutes or so—it seemed much longer—before searching for Eleanora. I found her in front of a bank of mirrors, checking out her new clothes. She wore a pair of designer jeans that fit like candy on an M&M. Her top was white and loose-fitting, and it hung off her shoulders. On her feet she wore sandals with a slight heel. I could tell by her face that she was pleased with the look, and I have to admit she was quite fetching. When she saw me behind her, she swayed slightly, still looking in the mirror, and sang,

"Some say, 'Baby, you're built for speed.'
Now ya put that all together,
Makes me everything a good man needs. . ."

Her voice rang through the department. Clerks looked up from transactions, ladies peered around racks of pink and beige culottes. All activity within view ceased.

"It's okay, she's a musician," I announced. Then to Eleanora, "Are you about finished?"

"All finished," she said with a satisfied smile. "Just let me collect my things."

On a chair nearby was a pile of clothes—another pair of jeans, several shirts, a dress or two, bras, and panties. She gathered it all up and held it against her chest as we walked to the nearest register. Midge, an older woman and some sort of manager, according to her name tag, had stepped forward to take care of the troublesome customer. She spread the clothes on the counter and began to ring them up. The younger clerk who had put Eleanora in that silly dress stood off to the side, eyeing us with a cool indifference. When Midge stretched out the bras to check the tags, I could not help taking a peek myself: 38D. She finished the tally and punched up the total.

"Three seventeen sixty-five," she said, looking at me. I looked at Eleanora. She looked at her feet.

"I seem to have forgotten my money, doll," she said. "If you can wait just a minute, I'll put these things back." Her disappointment was palpable. If it was fake, it was masterful.

I dug into my back pocket.

"Let's use this," I said to Midge, handing her my Visa card.

She bagged the clothes and we started to go. Suddenly, Eleanora stopped and reached into one of the bags. She pulled out a bra and tossed it to the young salesclerk. The girl made a clumsy grab for it, looping a strap around her wrist.

"If you try real hard," Eleanora said, "you might grow into it."

Out in the parking lot, Eleanora lit a cigarette and squeezed my upper arm, saying, "You should get out more often. That was fun."

CHAPTER 6

I don't know when I first realized that the best of life was probably behind me. But somewhere along the road I learned that patience, acceptance, and the simple desire to survive had to replace excitement, enthusiasm, the thrill of just being alive. It didn't happen at the supposed turning point of thirty. Gin and I didn't even marry till we were in our thirties, though we had known each other since high school. That extended courtship, I'm sure, was just another product of my inability to make a decision when making a decision was not crucial. Of course, we had both dated others during that time, none long-lasting, but it did not seem to matter. We knew we'd be together. I suppose some things are inevitable beyond death and taxes.

Nor was it after Gin's death, as a result of grief, that I first sensed the adventure was over. It happened sometime before, not one of those troubling middle-of-the-night insights that leave you staring at the ceiling, heart pounding, listening as the clock strikes three, four, five. It was so gradual as to be imperceptible at first, like the appearance of a few stray hairs in places they never existed before or the yellowing of the bathroom wallpaper.

It is not a depressing notion, but it's not particularly uplifting, either. As Zen followers are fond of saying, it just is.

And that's the hell of it.

*   *   *

My parents were never allowed to grow old. Their house would never smell like my grandparents' home—of mildew and perspiration and cooked peas. I was their only child and was subsequently overprotected. After a half-dozen miscarriages (some people never give up), my mother had me, Max and Helen Cooper's miracle.

*   *   *

Mom and Dad owned a pet-grooming service in St. Louis, where I grew up. It was a business that would eventually curl my teenage lip, but they were quite successful at it. Then suddenly they chucked it all, surprising absolutely everyone, saying they no longer found any joy in clipping doggy toenails and cleaning doggy ears, and they became Good Hope Messengers, as they were called, in Malawi.

Their message was simple: Believe in God, believe in yourself, believe in hard work and education, and good things will happen to you.

They both contracted encephalitis about three weeks after arriving, and my mom and dad died before they could get decent medical care. I was in grad school at the time and didn't know about it until their bodies arrived in New York and a man called asking if I were ever going to claim them. As if they were a package at the post office.

In a way, I envy them. They died together.

*   *   *

What's odd about it all is that I don't remember Dad or Mom ever talking about religious feeling of any sort. Only once did my mother come close, and it was when she sat on the edge of my bed explaining that yes, I would have to leave her the next morning to enter kindergarten.

But what would I do, I had asked, without her to protect me?

"Little boys like you have a spirit who watches them," she'd said, unintentionally spooking me more. Later that night, I woke her to say, "But what if mine is blind?"

"That's not possible," she'd said, "because a spirit without eyes is just a hole in the sky."

I never believed in such things.

Even the most determined hermit must find that there are some days he simply cannot avoid leaving the cave. I had let my car tag expire and decided to combine my trip to the license bureau with a run for groceries, cat food, and kitty litter. I also needed to have fixed a troublesome tooth that had begun waking me with pain. I suspected a root canal might be necessary.

Before I left for the day, I wanted to make sure Eleanora felt at home. I told her to feel free to watch TV, and I handed her the remote. She examined it, turned it over, fingered the numbers.

"Here's the ON button," I said, reaching over her shoulder and pressing it. Picture and sound popped on.

"My God," Eleanora said.

"What?"

"The colors," she said. "They're beautiful."

"Yeah," I said, thinking more about the dentist's chair and the long lines at the DMV. I showed her how to change channels and said I really had to go. She stared at the screen as she stepped back and sat down on the sofa. M. P. soon joined her, curling up on a pillow and shutting her eyes tight.

I left Eleanora transfixed, her fingers moving up and down the remote, through all the channels and back again and finally settling on *Oprah*

"Yeah, you go, girl," I heard her repeat as I pulled the door shut.

★   ★   ★

I returned home after five, arms full of groceries, mouth stuffed with gauze, and mood most foul. Eleanora met me at the door with a dour expression.

"I have something bad to tell you," she announced.

"Terrific," I said with tongue and lips two sizes too big. "What is it? The water heater explode again? You didn't let the cat out, did you?" I set the bags on a chair by the door and noticed an ashtray on the counter, stuffed with Pall Mall butts. A prodigious amount of puffing, even for her. I popped a Vicodin the dentist had prescribed and shoved the bottle in my pocket.

Eleanora produced from behind her back a compact disc, Duke Ellington doing Gershwin.

"I think I've ruined one of your little records."

"Little records?"

She held it up to my face.

"I can see it," I said. "What do you mean you ruined it? Those things are practically indestructible." I drooled and dabbed at my chin.

"I just tried to play it, baby," she said. She made me follow her to the stereo so she could re-create the crime. Unbelievably, she lifted the dust cover of the turntable, slipped the CD onto the spindle, turned on the power, and placed the needle on the disc. It slid quickly across with a horrible screech.

"Then I flipped the record," she said, "to see if the other side would play." She did just that as I stared, my packed mouth agape. The initial swirl of hydrocodone had reached my brain, accentuating the unreality of the display. I could think of nothing to say.

Eleanora removed the CD from the turntable and, in attempting to put it back in its case, cracked the lid. She sank heavily onto the sofa and covered her face with her hands.

"You've been nothing but straight up with me." The words came out between sobs. "And all I do is destroy your lovely home."

I sighed, took the disc from her, and inspected it. Both sides were marred by long, jagged scratches. It was shot.

"You haven't ruined anything," I said. "You just messed up a CD, one I got on sale anyway." She looked at me gratefully. What I didn't do was ask her how someone in the music business could be such a technological idiot around a stereo. From a druggy cloud I determined that with any more episodes like this, as a roommate Eleanora was history.

★   ★   ★

Later on, Eleanora helped me unpack the groceries—three jumbo jars of peanut butter, boxes of crackers, enough gourmet cat food to supply the Humane Society for a month, beer, and pipe cleaners. We laughed when I told Eleanora I didn't even like peanut butter, that I hoped she did.

"How many of those pills have you had?" she said. "Have any extra?"

We skipped dinner and ended up at the table in the Florida room, drinks in front of us—beer for me, straight bourbon for her—and she told me a little about her past. She was born in the East—where exactly she wouldn't say. (She had traveled enough to know that one place was pretty much like another.) She'd been married, was now divorced. She was lousy at picking men, she said, just like her mother had been. Her parents never married, and her father never lived under the same roof with her and her mother. For a while she lived with an aunt who smacked her around a good deal, and one night her great-grandmother died while holding her tight.

"They had to break the poor woman's arm to get me free," Eleanora said, dipping a finger into her drink and licking it.

"Jesus." I drained my beer and went for another one. "Go on," I said after hurrying back.

Later was a Catholic girls' school where punishment for even minor infractions was severe. For one offense that Eleanora refused to disclose, she was forced to pass around to the other girls a parcel of small gifts her mother had sent her, not being allowed to keep a single one for herself. Another time she was locked in a room overnight with a girl who had died earlier that day.

I looked hard into Eleanora's eyes—eyes that didn't look back at me but behind me or into me.

"Didn't anybody report these things?" I said.

Eleanora smiled.

"It's amazing," she said, "the pain a child will endure if she thinks she's supposed to."

It must have been the combination of beer and painkillers, but at that point the room faded, the lights growing dim and fuzzy. Eleanora faded, too, and for just a moment I thought I could see through her to the wooden blinds behind. I closed my eyes to clear the image, and when I opened them again, it was morning, and I stared at the fan whirling above my bed.

CHAPTER 7

Sometimes you pick a house, sometimes it seems to pick you, and other times you just end up with each other, like two desperate souls who fall together and pretend they're in love. For us and the bungalow on Twelfth Avenue North, it was definitely the latter. Gin's maternal grandmother—who'd recently died after a long tangle with diabetes—had owned the place, and on her death it passed to Gin's mother. Everyone knew what a *collector* Grandma had been, but the extent of her saving and hoarding, the sheer pathology of it, didn't reveal itself till we poked through the place after the funeral. Boxes, bags, racks of clothes, furniture, and old appliances reached the ceiling in every room. A narrow path led from bed to living room chair to front door, and that was the only walking space. You could barely call it walking, really; it was more of a sidling through crevices of cardboard, wood, and musty garments.

Gin and I, married just a year, were living in a cramped apartment, and Phyllis offered to sell us the place—exactly as it was—for a price we could afford. We could not have bought a house in Naples any other way.

I approached the massive cleanup like an earthmover. For Gin, it was a painstaking archaeological dig. This was, after all, her family history. My patience grew short as she picked through shoeboxes, examining coins and buttons; moved her fingertips over the backs of gaudy postcards; and tried on hats and sparkly evening gowns. I just wanted Grandma's stuff gone so we could make the place our own.

We had a weeklong yard sale, and the neighbors trickled in, more curious about the artifacts mounding in the drive than about us. But soon, a pitcher of iced tea arrived with Mrs. Solewecki, a six-pack with Mr. Solewecki, and ten helping hands with Paul and Kathy Foster and their brood. I bought buckets of fried chicken, and we passed them around and laughed uncomfortably like strangers trying to be friends often do.

And later, in the twilight, sitting on the ground beneath the Cuban laurel, ferns itching my elbows, I watched Virginia through a window, though she didn't know it. And I felt, for the first time in my life, what it was like to have a place to sink my teeth into, a place that I was responsible for and had to nourish.

The minutiae of a lifetime that Grandma Nessie had saved— much of it has spread across the country, but some we kept and absorbed into two new lives.

But this *stuff* lives on. And now, alone and surrounded by it, I finally understood the immeasurable value of these objects, the simple things that survive.

There is a crease in the fleshy part of some people's earlobes that is supposed to indicate an early death. I have that crease. In the weeks following Virginia's death, I obsessed over the thing, examining it in the mirror every afternoon, squeezing and twisting my earlobe to make it disappear. For a while I got a perverse delight out of hiding it with makeup I found in Virginia's vanity. I was fooling fate, I told myself. Not denying it, just tweaking its nose: Take that! After a while, thankfully, I lost interest in the game and by default made some sort of peace with my earlobes.

Eleanora had taken off again, to where I didn't know, and to do what I hadn't a clue. To get a singing gig, I hoped, since another mortgage payment was overdue and I could use whatever meager contribution she could make.

So I was again left to rattle around the house alone, something I was finding more difficult to do. I was sleeping even less than usual, and that left vast stretches of daytime with scant diversions other than vapid television, hide-and-seek with Mashed Potatoes, and pointless strolls around the block. God knows there was plenty to do around the house, but I had never been much good at noticing such things. For example, it might take a ceiling tile working loose and dropping on my head before I realized some maintenance was in order.

"Help me see with your eyes, Gin," I said aloud one afternoon as the silence, save the ticking of an anniversary clock, was about to drive me batty.

Although it still seems incredible, one of Virginia's aunts asked me, shortly after the memorial service, if I now regretted that Gin and I had put off having children. The cruelty of it aside, it was a difficult question.

Ours has become the great barren generation, men and women in their thirties and forties who do not have children of their own and probably never will. We were always more interested in our schooling, our travels, our creative endeavors—the unfinished novel, the second-rate poetry published in obscure little magazines, the master's thesis that rests undisturbed in the back wing of the college library where they keep the lights off to conserve electricity. We have always been a self-absorbed lot, maybe downright selfish, and as we approach middle age we are, if not exactly regretful, at least a little wistful about what might have been had we joined the timeless march. We are forever children to our parents, but we are parents to no one.

I was mulling this over, feeling sorry for myself, when Eleanora returned, late at night, and found me in my usual place on the pool deck.

"Good evening," she said quietly, this time not startling me, though I had not known she was there.

"Why so gloomy, baby?"

"Nothing. Everything," I said.

Eleanora sat on the edge of the pool. She wore a satiny dress, blue I thought, though it was dark, one I think she bought the day we went shopping. She took off her shoes and dangled her feet in the water, creating not a ripple.

"You need to get out of this house more," she said. "Have some fun, 'cause, honey, I think you're turning to stone."

I glared at the back of her head. Candor, in my opinion, has always been overrated.

"I don't remember asking for advice," I said.

"I've got eyes, doll, I can't help but see. Look around. This house is like a shrine, an abandoned shrine. You think I don't see how you put those bottles and glasses back on the shelf in exactly the same place they came from? Old magazines stay stacked perfectly on the coffee table. Have you taken out a newspaper this year? Baby, the only thing piled higher is the leaves on the bottom of this pool you never swim in. And I know you go into that room I'm staying in and put everything back where it was before I got here. I moved a speck of dust, so I know."

I was burning holes in the back of Eleanora's new dress. She turned to face me, and all I could make out were her eyes.

"Sugar, it ain't good," she said.

"Sugar, baby, honey," I said mockingly, launching myself out of the chair and striding past Eleanora toward the Florida room. "You talk like a bad old movie."

CHAPTER 8

Tragedy threads the tapestry of jazz. So does a great appreciation of the here and now, because it's all you may get, brother. You can hear it in the music; it's why the best jazz recordings
are often live performances, done in smoky bars in one take.
More than simply entertainment or background, each improvisa-
tion is a holy person's call to find the nearest beautiful thing—
whatever it is—and embrace it while you can.

Listen to Miles Davis's *Kind of Blue* and you'll hear it flowing
unmistakably through every player. There's Cannonball Adderley,
the jovial fat man with the soft sax, the high school teacher who
left the classroom to find his heaven, gone before middle age.
Same with piano man Bill Evans, the best of his day, and the
longest suicide in history, a friend called him. And the great John
Coltrane, who was a holy man for real and who died, some say of
genius, long before his first gray hair. But one afternoon, brought
together with Davis, they found themselves speaking the language
of God, and they recorded it to keep it forever.

I slept for just a few hours, but Eleanora beat me out of bed.
The woman certainly didn't need much downtime; I had never

caught her sleeping. That morning I found her in the kitchen, again watching the coffeemaker dribble its contents into the pot.

"That thing sure fascinates you," I said

She looked up with a poker face. "I daresay, Mr. Cooper, it is the greatest invention since the Victrola." She spoke without inflection, like a robot. She was getting me back.

"I'm sorry I snapped at you last night," I said. "I've been a little touchy lately. For a long time, actually." I pulled two mugs from the cabinet overhead.

"Don't you worry about it," she said. "Here, let me." Waiting till the last drip of coffee had dropped into the carafe, she gingerly removed the pot and slowly poured. "If you don't mind, I'll have a little something extra in mine," she said. She uncapped a nearly empty bottle of bourbon she had brought in from the Florida room and poured some into her cup. I arched an eyebrow but said nothing. Then she persuaded me to have some myself.

Later, as I sat on the living room sofa, Eleanora in a wicker chair with Mashed Potatoes curled in her lap, I made what for me was a major announcement.

"You might have been right last night. Maybe I ought to get out more." I fingered my coffee cup, now cold, and, like an eighth-grader with bad acne, couldn't bring myself to meet Eleanora's big cow eyes.

I said, "I think I'd like to rent a canoe at the Conservancy this afternoon, paddle around the mangroves. It's something we haven't—I haven't—done for a long time. Would you like to come?"

I glanced up at Eleanora. She stared at me, mouth slightly open.

"Hello?" I said.

She blinked.

"A canoe? You mean the boat kind?" She made a paddling motion with her hands.

"Yeah."

She broke into a hearty laugh, long and deep and genuine. I had not heard her laugh like that before, and it delighted me. Tears came to her eyes. M. P., annoyed at the sudden jostling, leaped to the floor.

"That didn't strike me as especially funny," I said, holding back a smile.

"You Tarzan, me Eleanora," she said and broke up again.

"Well, forget it," I said, placing my cup on an end table and crossing my legs defensively. "I'll go by myself." As I started to rise, Eleanora put her hand up to stop me.

"But honey," she said, all phony innocence, "I haven't a thing to wear." She laughed again, and I resisted the urge to touch her hair.

We stood before Virginia's open closet, Eleanora with wide-eyed curiosity, me with crawling anxiety.

"May I?" Eleanora said.

I nodded, and she began to push the clothes along the rack, holding out one outfit for inspection, then another. A mildewy smell wafted from the clothes, a pungent reminder of just how long Gin had been gone.

"I'll wait out here till you find something," I said, quickly leaving the bedroom and retreating to the kitchen. I poured myself another coffee and bourbon and paced the living room as I sipped my drink. Finally, Eleanora emerged. She was dressed in khaki shorts and shirt and old gym shoes. Though Gin had been smaller than Eleanora, she had always bought her clothes a size or two too big so they'd hang loose and baggy, bohemian-like. It was her only artsy pretense.

"Ungawah," she said and placed her hands on her hips.

"Everything seems to fit," I said. "The shoes feel all right?"

"A little tight," she said. "But I can untie them."

Perhaps sensing my discomfort, she suddenly got very quiet.

"Then let's do it," I said. My enthusiasm for the outing was disappearing rapidly.

It was mid-July, so most of the German tourists had gone home, as had the old couples from Ohio. The tranquillity of the preserve would be undisturbed by folks snapping pictures of pelicans and talking too loudly about their last round of golf. It was the best time of year in Naples, provided you could handle the heat and mosquitoes. That was tough; both were fierce.

I collected our cushions and paddles and steadied the canoe while Eleanora climbed gingerly in front.

"Can you swim?" I said.

"Like an icebox," Eleanora said.

I told her not to worry, that I had no intention of dumping the boat. If I were going to be safari guide, I was going to do it right.

I stepped into the back of the canoe, causing Eleanora to clutch the sides, and untied us from the dock. We were off.

I paddled slowly through the tea-colored water, trying not to disturb things as yet unseen. I remembered that it took some time to adjust when you came to a place like this. You needed to change your way of looking and listening, concentrate on a detail, and the whole would appear. On Sunday mornings Virginia and I would often come here. Or stroll the boardwalk through Corkscrew Swamp, binoculars and water jug in hand. Or go to the beach and look for fresh turtle nests so we could erase the mother turtles' tracks and fool raccoons. Gin would sometimes ask if I felt guilty that we weren't in church. I never did because in a way I felt we were.

Crabs clacked as they scuttled up and down mangrove roots. Eleanora picked up her paddle, holding it like a baseball player laying down a bunt, dipped it in the water and began to stroke. Backward.

"Why don't you just relax and enjoy the scenery?" I said. "You're my guest today. I'll do the work."

She put down her paddle, and I scanned the tangled shore, looking for some creature of interest to show Eleanora. We rounded a bend and a great blue heron took flight, a fish impaled on its beak.

"Oh, look there," Eleanora said, pointing at it. I was happy that she might be enjoying this.

Then I spotted what I was really looking for—a gator, three or four feet long, sunning itself on a log. I turned the canoe and paddled toward it.

"Alligator," I said.

"Horseshit," said Eleanora.

"There," I said. "Straight ahead." I lifted my paddle and we glided slowly toward the log.

"Sweet baby Jesus," Eleanora said. Then she stood, turned around, and began an awkward scramble toward my end of the canoe.

"Eleanora, no," I shouted. "This isn't a flat-bottomed boat." I shifted back and forth, trying to counterbalance her movement, but it was too late. I dropped my paddle in the water and over we went.

I popped up quickly, spitting brackish water, and looked around. The gator was gone from the log, and there was no sign of Eleanora. I called her name once, twice, three times. No response. Only the hum of a thousand insects clustering around my face.

"Eleanora," I yelled, then dove beneath the surface. Waterlogged shoes made swimming almost impossible, and the water was too dark to see through. I popped up again, panicked.

"Eleanora," I screamed.

From the left shore I heard her voice.

"It's hot as Hades, a lady's not safe in his arms . . .," she sang, her voice swallowed by the forest. She stood on a hump of mangrove root, clutching a branch above her head. My FSU cap sat askew on her head. She laughed.

"What the hell's so funny?" I said, glaring at her as I spit out salty water. I swam to the overturned canoe, reached underneath for a crossbar, and sidestroked with it over to where Eleanora was perched, looking delighted.

"You do know how to show a girl a good time, baby," she said.

I stood up in the shallows and righted the canoe.

"Madam," I said, pointing to her seat in front. She climbed in, and we headed back to the dock. One paddle must've drifted away, and I'd lost my sunglasses, but that was all. I was strangely serene, and I noticed something remarkable.

"Eleanora, do you walk on water?" From Reeboks to baseball cap, she seemed dry. She made an exaggerated gesture of feeling her clothing.

"I must be wash and wear, doll," she said.

When we got home, Mashed Potatoes was all over me, sniffing and licking my damp, fishy clothes. I squished in my shoes as I went to undress and shower. I don't know why, but I felt I had just accomplished something.

That night Eleanora and I got shamelessly drunk. Early on I told her that if she were going to spend much time in South Florida, she had to get hip (I actually said that) to the flora and fauna here. That while some creatures were certainly to be avoided, a baby alligator was not one of them. She said that outside of dogs, she'd never been too keen on animals, that she saw only rats where she grew up. She said she'd make an effort, though, if it would make me happy. The day and the booze had made us compadres, and we talked like old friends instead of unlikely roommates.

Later we played jazz CDs, and Eleanora stood me up to dance.

As we swayed in the living room, M. P. looked on, puzzled, and Eleanora said, "You got a rusty hinge somewhere, honey. Loosen up. It's like dancing with an ironing board."

A few more vodkas and orange juice and my hinge was so oiled I couldn't stand up. I awoke the next morning on the sofa. A distant ringing in my head soon turned to pounding.

CHAPTER 9

"Casey, I know you're in there. I saw you sleeping on the sofa."

It was my mother-in-law, an incorrigible window-peeper. One Sunday morning years ago, when Gin and I were ignoring the phone and the door, she caught us, through a crack in the blinds, in bed, her daughter's ankles draped over my shoulders. Even that had not cured her.

"What is it, Phyllis?" I called.

"Open the door, will you? Please?"

I struggled to get up, pressing a palm against my forehead. I flattened the back of my hair and straightened my shirt. I slipped off my remaining shoe.

"Good morning, Phyllis," I said, shielding my eyes against the light. "Is something wrong?"

"You look like hell. Can I come in?"

I opened the screen door for her, then turned and walked, sort of, to the kitchen. I cursed myself for forgetting to set the coffeemaker the night before.

"Coffee?" I said, filling the carafe with water.

She said she'd had some.

"Have a seat. I'll be just a minute." With my elbows on the counter, I watched the slow trickle into the pot.

After I had poured a cup, black and bracing, I found Phyllis in the Florida room, looking at the table that held two glasses, an empty orange juice jug, and two half-empty bottles of vodka.

"Looks like you had quite a time of it with your company last night," she said, a real Columbo at deciphering clues.

"It wasn't exactly company." I prayed that Eleanora would not come out until I'd explained.

"Family, then?" she said. She knew I had no family in town.

"No. I've got a roommate," I said.

Phyllis inspected my face for a moment.

"Well that's probably a good idea," she finally said. "It's not healthy to be shut up alone all the time." She looked toward the hallway. "I hope I didn't wake him."

She hadn't minded waking me.

"What's his name?" she said.

I took a deep breath. "Eleanora."

She frowned.

"You certainly didn't waste much time, did you? I guess that explains why nobody's seen much of you."

I explained that we were roommates, nothing more. Phyllis looked skeptical, then shook her head.

"It's not kosher," she said. "What will people think?"

I told her how little I cared, but I was beginning to sweat, a droplet sliding down my jaw and landing on my chest.

"When do I get to meet this Eleanor, then?"

"Right now," I said. I didn't need this, not this morning. I marched down the hall, motioning her to follow. M. P. scurried out of our way and under a chair. At Eleanora's door I paused, listening. She could not have slept through the booming of Phyllis's voice, and I hoped that when she came out, she had the good sense not to throw around the "baby" and "honey" and "doll."

I knocked lightly—*Shave-and-a-haircut*—and called her name. A knock came in response: *Two-bits*.

"I'd like you to meet someone. Are you decent?" I said, immediately fearing her possible response to that question. Not another sound. I knocked again and then slowly turned the doorknob. What Phyllis and I found was an empty room, bed made, Virginia's khaki shorts and shirt draped neatly across a chair, Reeboks placed underneath.

I opened the closet and saw only the junk that had always been there. I yanked open dresser drawers and dug through the contents. Eleanora had taken everything she owned—the navy blue dress she had arrived in, the clothes from Burdine's, her shoes, everything. Either that, or she had hidden them somewhere. I sat on the bed, bewildered.

"You heard her answer me, didn't you?" I said.

"I heard you knock."

Phyllis sat down next to me, put an arm around me and pulled me to her.

"Oh, Casey," she said, her voice subdued. "Casey, I'm so sorry. We all miss her very much, you know that, don't you? You're not alone in this."

What could I say? I had no idea what was happening.

"Why don't you have supper with Bob and me tonight?" she said. "We can all talk. It's been too long since we've talked."

Barely above a whisper I said that dinner would be fine. Phyllis stood up, patted my head, and told me to get some sleep.

That, too, I thought, would be fine.

But who the hell had knocked?

The smoke from Bob's cigarette (Didn't anyone try to quit anymore?) was reawakening my hangover. Bob was in swim trunks, as he always was when home, winter or summer, and his wet hair was slicked behind his ears. He was alarmingly tanned, his rough face a perpetual scowl that had intimidated the hell out of me when Gin and I started dating. I had long since learned, however, that his expression had nothing to do with his mood.

"I want to level with you, Casey," he said, pounding out one cigarette and lighting another. "We've known each other too long for anything else." He took a deep drag. Dramatic pauses had always been part of his conversational style.

"Phyllis was alarmed at what she saw at your house today."

I nodded. It was far too hot to be sitting outdoors, especially next to a fired-up barbecue grill. I wished that we could take this inside.

"People grieve in different ways," Bob went on. "There is no right or wrong about it. For several weeks after the accident, Phyllis and I even talked to Virginia like she was still with us, right in the same goddamn room."

"I still do that," I said.

Bob looked down at his hands, one cupping the cigarette. I tried to be inconspicuous as I snorted smoke away from my face.

"The thing is," he said, "don't let it eat you up. We all have to go on and live what's left of our lives. Without Virginia."

My eyes began to burn, and I blamed it on the smoke.

Bob reached behind him and pulled something from the pocket of a shirt draped across a chair. It was a business card.

Vincent Gonzalez, it read. *Licensed Psychotherapist. FL Lic. No. 001692. Adults, Children, Families. Special Interest In: Self-Esteem, Stress, Anxiety, Depression, Grief.*

Someone had underlined "Grief."

"You remember Vince," Bob said. I did. I'd met him at one of Bob and Phyllis's parties a few years back. He had seemed overly sincere but likable, with eyes that moved independently of each other, like a gecko's. He had taught with Bob at Naples High until the kids drove him over the brink and he returned to grad school. Now he counseled nearly every teacher in town, inspiring several I knew to leave the profession and open pottery shops.

I fingered the business card, flexed it, read it three or four times—anything to avoid Bob's earnest gaze. I had been down this path before. Bob knew that I had seen a psychiatrist in the weeks after the accident and that we had not gotten on at all.

"I called Vince this afternoon," he said. "He remembered you and said he'd be glad to talk. Hope you don't mind, but I made an appointment for you."

I turned the card over and read, *1:00 P.M. Thursday.*

"See him," Bob said as he came over and hugged me like Phyllis had. My cheek pressed against his sticky skin. "Virginia wouldn't want to see you like this."

Gently, I tried to pull away, but he hugged me tighter, saying, "You know, you've always been like a son to us."

That was a load of crap, but at that moment, I appreciated it. When you suspect that you're losing your mind, a little sympathy goes a long way.

Dr. Gonzalez's office was located in one of those new breeds of strip mall, the kind that attempt an upscale look, with stuccoed exteriors and small courtyards with tiny fountains in the center. His office, which he shared with several other therapists, sat between H&R Block and Banana Republic.

Dr. Gonzalez met me at the receptionist's desk, cheerful but, thankfully, subdued. He led me to a room with two folding chairs, a long table, and a large mirror embedded in the wall. He sat me down and said he'd be with me momentarily. Then he left, pulling the door to but not closing it completely. The walls were bare except for a small sign beneath the mirror that stated, "You may be observed while in this room." Okay, so the mirror was one-way glass. I moved to the window and looked out.

Mockingbirds in a nearby tree were engaged in some sort of courtship ritual, with one raising its wings and squawking, the other dancing back and forth on a branch below. Either that or it was a fight.

I looked over at the mirror, managing a wan smile and a wave and then wondered if that might constitute usual behavior.

Finally, Gonzalez returned, smiling, carrying a sheaf of papers and a pencil. I tried to lock onto one eye or the other as he talked.

★   ★   ★

"This is a standard preevaluation form," he said. "Nothing unusual. But we have to have it on file." He set it on the table and motioned for me to sit down.

"Take your time and answer honestly." He patted my shoulder and left again.

The form was a list of questions, ninety-nine of them, and my response to each was to be "Strongly Disagree," "Disagree," "Don't Know," "Agree," or "Yes! That's Me!" I picked up the pencil and tried to forget that someone was undoubtedly watching me do *this,* too.

Statement 1: "I consider myself a happy person."

An easy one. I checked "Don't Know."

Statement 2: "People are generally fair and honest." It was clear already that this test needed a wider range of possible responses. After several minutes I checked "Agree."

It went on like that for fifteen or twenty statements, assessing my general view of the world to determine if I was a raving paranoiac. But wouldn't a paranoiac lie on such a test? So wouldn't I prove myself sane by answering as an honest paranoid? I shook my head vigorously to derail this train of thought, aware that that was duly noted on the other side of the mirror.

Then the test got strange.

Statement 24: "I often feel like a puppet, with someone else working the strings." I crossed out the list of responses and wrote in the margin, "Literally or metaphorically?"

Statement 73: "There are evil people inside of me trying to get out." Fortunately, I could strongly disagree with that. Whatever evil was inside of me was perfectly content to stay there and do its work. I provided it with such a comfy home.

The evaluation completed, I slid the papers away from me, put the pencil down, and shrugged toward the mirror. I had been trying hard not to, but I was really getting the creeps.

Dr. Gonzalez came in, smiled, took my evaluation, and left again. Twenty or thirty long minutes later he returned, pulled up a chair a little too close to me, and sat down.

"Well, Casey," he said, patting a folder bearing my name, "your results indicate that you're not schizophrenic. If, of course, you answered honestly."

I shifted a bit and said that I had.

"But there clearly is something troubling you. Troubling you enough that your in-laws . . . (cough) . . . your former in-laws say you have invented an imaginary roommate, a new friend or partner, so to speak."

I interrupted. It was my therapy, after all.

"I don't know what Phyllis or Bob may have told you," I said. "But I have a roommate. She comes and goes at weird hours, I know, and she takes everything she owns each time. But I swear to you I'm not making her up."

He nodded and eyed me, his roving eyes suddenly reminding me of those slow-moving beacons that announce the grand opening of a new department store.

"What's her name?" he said.

"Eleanora."

"Last name?"

"That I don't know."

He nodded, opened my folder, and slowly turned pages.

"We've been out," I went on. "We went shopping. I took her canoeing. She tipped the boat over and didn't even get wet . . ."

I knew immediately I'd screwed up. Gonzalez looked at me with genuine concern.

After a long pause he said, "You're drinking for two. That's what Phyllis told me. She said you pour two glasses, then drink from both. Is that right? She said you answered the door feeling poorly from having drunk too much."

"Yeah, sometimes I drink for two," I said. "But I damned sure don't need two glasses to do it. The night before Phyllis came by—incidentally, she could use a little therapy herself—Eleanora drank me under the table. We were just kicking back after our canoe trip."

"The one where she didn't get wet after falling in the water," Gonzalez noted, pressing the eraser of his pencil into his lower lip.

"I didn't say she fell in," I said. I got up and walked over to the window.

"But the boat tipped over?"

"Yes."

"And you fell in?"

"Yes."

"And she was in the same boat?"

I sighed. "Look," I said, "there are a lot of things about this woman that are unusual. I'll admit that. And there's a lot about her I don't know."

He nodded again and nibbled the eraser. He pointed for me to return to my seat. "The loss of a spouse is perhaps the most devastating thing that anyone can experience," he said. "It can overload even the strongest nervous system with a host of competing emotions, some of which you may try to suppress."

I put my elbows on my knees and looked down at my hands.

"Frankly, Casey, your reaction to your loss disturbs me. It is extreme. I believe you have fantasized an entirely new partner to partly compensate for your loss."

"I told you that's not the case," I said, my voice rising.

Gonzalez continued, unruffled.

"Casey, let's pretend we're detectives and review the evidence," he said. "I'm trying to help you. Okay, you say she lives with you, but she has no possessions in the house, not even, presumably, a toothbrush."

I gave a slight nod.

"You said she arrives at odd hours, usually at night—after you've been drinking or dozing—and often without making a sound."

I stared at the floor.

"You don't know her last name, where she's from, or where she works. Finally, you say she tipped a boat over and either fell in without getting wet or walked on water."

The room spun as it began to sink in that the doctor, Phyllis, and Bob might be right.

"You are obviously depressed," he said, "severely depressed, and, I think, a very real threat to yourself. There may be more at work here as well, and I am concerned."

My heart scudded.

"It seems to me that for whatever reason, you have tried, in this imaginary Eleanora, to re-create your wife. We need to find out why you feel this need so deeply and arrest it before it spirals out of control—which it will likely do if left untreated."

Gonzalez put a fatherly hand on my knee.

"I sense that the root of this problem is something you've not yet revealed," he said.

How right the good doctor was. But I wasn't about to reveal it. Not to Dr. Gonzalez, not to Phyllis, not to Bob, not to anybody. I couldn't tell them that I'd been responsible for Gin's death.

CHAPTER 10

I didn't go straight home after leaving the doctor's office. I was afraid to. I was afraid the walls would close in on me, afraid of what I might hear or see, or who might drop by. Maybe now the bungalow hosted a bevy of ghosts.

Dr. Gonzalez had found my case beyond his ken, and he referred me to a psychiatrist. I was in such serious shape that they had scheduled an emergency session for me the following morning. Gonzalez had also said something about hospitalization, but by then I was catching a word only here or there. My brain refused to process the undeniable: I was really fucked up, and everybody thought so.

I drove to the beach and, still in my good clothes from the appointment, sat down in the sand and looked out at the Gulf. A couple of high school kids flinging a Frisbee looked at me, then looked at each other and smiled. As if I were nuts. I could picture it painted in neon on my forehead. I leaned forward, chin in hand, and let the sun burn into my scalp for a good long time. The Frisbee throwers left, the old folks arrived with their lawn chairs to watch the sunset, and I realized that Mashed Potatoes' dinner was several hours late. As she would tell you if she could, her dinner waits for no man, not even one who is losing his mind. So I got up, brushed off the sand, and headed home.

I could hear M. P.'s complaints before I put the key in the lock. When I opened the door she berated me soundly.

"I'm sorry," I said, bending to rub her head. "I got tied up." I opened a can of tuna as consolation and spooned half onto her plate.

Before I'd left his office, Dr. Gonzalez had given me the number of the crisis hotline and his home phone number. I was to call one or the other, at any hour, if Eleanora reappeared. With a *Peanuts* magnet that read "Good Grief," I stuck the numbers to the freezer door at eye level.

I opened the refrigerator, took out a beer, and popped it. I took a sip, then rushed to the sink to spit it out. It tasted like a mouthful of pennies. My stomach churned and I broke a sweat. I needed to talk, so I picked up the phone to call—whom? I couldn't load any more onto Bob and Phyllis, and I sure didn't feel like starting the story from scratch for some counseling volunteer stuck on phone duty at the crisis center.

I turned instead to my best friend since Virginia died. I scooped up Mashed Potatoes as she gave herself a postprandial wash. She purred as she lay draped over my right arm, and I walked with her to the living room sofa. There we sat until all daylight evaporated, and I stroked her dense fur and lost myself in the electrostatic sprinkle of sparks.

*   *   *

Much later I awoke, jerking my head from the armrest of the sofa.

"That's it," I said. I jumped up, turned on a lamp, and went to the stereo. I flipped through my CD collection until I came to *Duke Ellington Plays Gershwin,* the one Eleanora had tried to play on the turntable. I ripped off the broken cover, plucked out the disc, and flashed it under the light. It was stupidly, wonderfully, beautifully scratched. Scarred all to hell. I let out a whoop, tossed the CD on the sofa, and rushed to Eleanora's room. I pulled Virginia's shirt and shorts—the ones Eleanora had borrowed—from the chair and inspected them, went through the pockets. Nothing, not a coin or gum wrapper or ball of lint. I picked up the shoes and looked them over, pulled out the tongues, shook them. I turned them over, and stuck to the sole of the left one was a piece of a leaf—the leathery tip of a mangrove leaf, barely moist.

Imaginary friend, my ass!

I picked up M. P. and planted a big kiss on her head. She squirmed free.

I went to the kitchen and pulled down Dr. Gonzalez's card. I checked the time—3:38 A.M.—but decided to call anyway. It rang four times and then the answering machine picked up. So much for the home phone number.

"Dr. Gonzalez, this is Casey," I said. "I'm calling to cancel my appointment for tomorrow and all the rest of it. I may be screwed up in a lot of ways, but I'm not crazy. I've got proof. But thanks for your help. Really. Bye."

★   ★   ★

So Eleanora existed: She walked, she talked, she sang off-key. But that didn't answer all of the questions.

A month or so later I had to leave the house, again not by choice but out of necessity. I had to visit the city utilities office, Florida Power and Light, and the cable company to plead or negotiate so they wouldn't cut off my services. I was several payments behind to all of them but took with me enough cash to make serious dents in what I owed.

So I endured, calmly, the humiliation I knew they had to dish out before they would cut a deal. All but the cable company. The service manager there took as a "disconnect fee" the twenty dollars I laid on the table and sent me away. Losing cable TV was no big deal. All I watched were baseball games, and the players were on strike again anyway. I was a little upset about the twenty, though.

When I pulled into the carport of the bungalow, I noticed a sheet of paper stuffed behind the screen door. Guys were always coming around and leaving coupons for a free car wash with a fill-up or one dollar off a large pizza. Such jobs in Naples were plentiful, good jobs almost nonexistent. I had given up one of the few.

This paper, however, was no coupon. I took it out into the sunlight to read it.

Notice, it read, *from the Collier County Health Department in conjunction with the City of Naples. It has come to our attention that someone on these premises, in violation of City Ordinance No. 0019.1a, has been feeding Muscovy ducks. As these ducks, by a majority vote of the Naples City Council, have been deemed a public nuisance, you are violating the law by providing them sustenance.*

Providing them sustenance? This was rich. It went on.

This notice constitutes First Warning. *Continued violations will result in a maximum fine of $50 for the first offense, $100 for each subsequent offense. Acknowledgment of this official notice by mail is advised.* It was signed *Woody Woodward, City Manager,* and designed so it could be folded into thirds, stamped, and returned.

*   *   *

The Muscovy duck controversy had become a huge local issue the previous summer when angry senior citizens approached the city council and demanded that it do something about the ubiquitous begging birds or they would take matters into their own hands and start bashing ducks with golf clubs. A gaggle of duck supporters soon emerged, and the two sides had red-faced, screaming arguments in front of the council several consecutive sessions. The council finally hit upon a compromise that made it illegal to feed or otherwise encourage the ducks to live long and happy lives, but they could not be killed outright. The council's heart, however, was clearly with those citizens who found it a disruption of paradise to clean duck shit off their Lincoln Town Cars. With a final wink and a smile, the mayor assured the assembly that if a duck were found bludgeoned by a nine iron, the death would be viewed as accidental.

★   ★   ★

Still puzzled as to why I got the notice, I unlocked the front door and went inside. A light was on in the spare bedroom.

"Eleanora?" I said. I hoped to see her.

"Shhhh," came the response.

I walked down the hallway and peered in. Eleanora sat on one of the twin beds, wearing that navy blue dress, her travel outfit. She gently stroked M. P., who lay on her back, eyes shut, kneading the air in pure bliss. Eleanora cooed to her softly, *"A foggy day . . . in London town . . . had me low . . . had me down . . ."*

"Well hello," I said.

"Hi there," she said, not looking up from the cat.

When it became obvious that she thought no explanation was necessary, I said, "Do you know the trouble you've caused me with your disappearing act?"

She looked up but continued rubbing M. P. "Trouble's my given name, honey. But you'll understand me someday, inscrutable as I am." She winked.

I sat down across from her, on the other bed. She continued her lullaby: *"The British Museum . . . had lost its charm . . ."*

"My in-laws think I made you up," I said.

A flawless segue in her lullaby:

"I say I'll move the mountains / And I'll move the mountains / If

he wants them out of the way / 'Crazy,' He calls me / Sure I'm crazy / Crazy in love, I'd say . . ."

I smiled. "I like that," I said.

"Thank you," she said softly. She then stared at me until I became uncomfortable.

"Where have you been? Or is that none of my business?"

"Working, doll," she said. "That reminds me . . ." She stood up and reached into a pocket of her dress. I caught the scent of the gardenia in her hair, and it made my toes tingle. Out of the pocket she pulled a handful of crumpled bills, several hundreds and a few twenties.

"I hope this will cover my stay for a while," she said. "And anything else I manage to break."

Embarrassed but grateful, I picked up the bills.

"Thanks."

An awkward silence followed, and I moved next to Eleanora, reaching to pet Mashed Potatoes. She awoke and grumbled at my touch.

"I was worried about you," I finally said.

"That's a waste of energy, love. Worry about yourself," she said.

I collapsed backward on the bed. "Oh, not you too," I groaned. "I'm fine. Really."

"Uh huh. And I'm the secretary of agriculture," she said.

Edgy and wanting to change the topic, I picked up the notice from the city manager that I'd left lying on the other bed.

"Do you know anything about this?" I said, handing her the paper. A stupid way to make conversation, considering.

She read it, brow scrunched, then looked at me.

"You said I should take more of an interest in wildlife. So I tried. I saw a duck—real homely duck—in the driveway, got a few pieces of bread from the icebox, and tossed him some. Oh, and Casey," she said, eyes widening, "suddenly there were ducks everywhere. They flew in by the dozens, maybe hundreds, their wings beating like a typhoon. I had to run for my ever-lovin' life."

Her face had become so childlike and full of wonder that I wanted to hug her. Instead, I laughed.

"I wish I'd seen that," I said. Then, "I've missed you. Missed having you around, I mean."

★   ★   ★

Later, in the den, I took the notice from Woody Woodward, city manager, wrote "Eat me" at the bottom, folded it into thirds, and put a stamp on it.

CHAPTER 11

That night I dreamed of Virginia again. I had gone into the kitchen and there she sat, atop the refrigerator. I used to playfully put her there on those wonderful Saturday nights when we were at school. She would then promise all manner of erotic delights if I would get her down. Then we would make love on the mattress we had dragged out into the living room of our tiny apartment. We would spend the rest of the night looking out at the treetops and the sky and talking about how we expected our lives to turn out.

In my dream she wore a long white winter nightgown, laced to the neck. She smiled, spread her legs slightly, and reached out for me to help her down. I held her by the waist, and she rested her hands on my shoulders.

"Watch the fan," she said, still smiling, glancing up at the whirling blades on the ceiling, and I recalled, without alarm, that she had been nearly decapitated in the accident. An orderly at the hospital had made that announcement in goggle-eyed amazement as he left the room where they had taken her.

She slid effortlessly off the refrigerator and into my arms, wrapping her legs around my waist. I carried her to our room and we fell onto the bed laughing. We kissed, and I felt the swell and lust of deprivation as we pressed against each other. I untied the gown at her neck, revealing a thumb-width scar traveling from ear to ear. I licked and nibbled the length of it, then opened the gown to her waist. She sat up and slipped out of it. We made love for a long time, but without climax, then lay quietly holding each other, her head on my shoulder.

"I wish you didn't have to go," I said.

"I do too," she said. A warm droplet hit my chest and rolled off my ribs.

When I awoke, in my dream, I was happy to see the silent sleeping form still next to me, covered to the top of her head.

"You didn't leave," I said, touching her arm.

She rolled over to reveal the face of Eleanora. I tried to scream and covered my eyes.

"Casey," she said.

"No."

"Casey, look at me."

I moved my hand from my face. Eleanora, eyes blank like the eyes of a death stare, reached out to touch my cheek. Instinctively, I snapped my head back.

"Don't touch me," I said. "I'm afraid."

"Casey," she said, "we're all of one. You, me, Virginia. You'll know that by and by."

Then I woke up for real, clammy, heart racing. Someone was knocking on my door.

"Casey," Eleanora said. I froze. "Casey, come quick."

I jumped out of bed, pulled on some shorts, and opened the door. A noxious odor swept in, provoking a primal fear.

"Where is it?" I said.

Eleanora pointed across the hall into her room, where an over-stuffed chair at the foot of the bed danced in flames. I ran down the hall to get a throw rug from the living room, returned with it to the guest room, and looked for Eleanora, waving away smoke with both hands. She was not there. By now the flames had licked the curtains and they flared like a match. I ripped them down and threw them to the floor, covering them with the rug and stamping. I tossed the rug over the chair and rushed it out of the house and into the driveway.

When I got back to the guest room, Eleanora sat on the edge of the bed, rocking back and forth. In her arms she cradled M. P., who lay motionless.

"I was having a smoke," she said. "And then I got to dreaming and wishing, and next thing I know, I'd forgotten all about smoking and . . . "

"Oh, no."

I put my hand on M. P.'s chest. It was still warm but not rising and falling. Gently, I took her from Eleanora and drove dangerously fast to the veterinarian.

When I delivered M. P. to the vet's assistant, my hands trembled.

"There was a fire," I said.

The assistant nodded. "We'll do what we can," she said.

"She's all I've got," I said, embarrassed that my voice caught. But it didn't matter. The woman had already taken M. P. away, leaving me alone in the waiting room.

When she returned, she said she'd telephone when the vet had finished. I told her I would rather wait right there, if she didn't mind. I said I thought it would be better if M. P. knew I was nearby.

"If you wish," she said, and disappeared again.

★　　★　　★

I sat in the empty reception area and flipped through some magazines. Too fidgety to sit down, I walked around the counter and looked down the hallway.

"I'm going to walk around outside," I said, hoping someone would hear me. A door opened and closed out of sight, and the assistant appeared around a corner, took my elbow, and ushered me back to the reception desk.

"She's getting some oxygen," she said. "Do we have your permission to do whatever else is necessary?"

I nodded.

"And it would be best if you stayed out here," she said, and walked quickly back down the hall.

★   ★   ★

I walked down busy Highway 41 toward a nearby 7-Eleven. It was September, so the heat and humidity were staggering, and by the time I'd made the short trip, my shirt was soaked and my head pounded. With some hesitation I opened a cooler and took out a tall Bud. When I set it on the counter, the clerk glanced at the clock behind him. It was ten after nine in the morning. When I realized I had only a dollar in my wallet, I charged it.

I walked behind the store to find quieter streets. Self-consciously, I opened the beer and took a long swallow. I wanted to stay within sight of the clinic in case they needed me for something. Several hours later, as I was counting the tiles from one wall of the waiting room to the other, the vet emerged with M. P.'s travel kennel.

"Smoke inhalation usually kills quickly," he said, "but she still has a faint pulse and is breathing, though it's very shallow."

He told me what all they had done to try to bring her around, but I peered into the kennel for a clue of my own. A lump of fur with dull eyes stared back at me.

"I can't in good conscience let you leave here too hopeful," the vet said. "Keep her warm and comfortable tonight, let her drink if she can, but other than that, it's out of our hands, my friend."

I paid them with plastic and thanked them several times.

*   *   *

Eleanora pulled open the front door as soon as my car hit the driveway.

"What's the news?" she said, bending to look in the crate.

There was already enough guilt and regret in the house for all of us. I hesitated a moment and then said, "She's fine. Just needs to sleep a little bit. She'll be good as new in the morning."

Eleanora exhaled heavily

"That's swell, Casey," she said. She held the screen door as I carried the case in. I set it carefully on the dining table and went to the hall closet, pulling out a cardboard box and emptying it of old college notebooks. I padded it with a blanket and pillow from my bed—Gin's old pillow—then carried the box to the bathroom and placed it in the shower under the window, where M. P. loved to sleep. I unbolted the top from the kennel so that I could lift her out and carried the limp creature like a birthday cake to the box. After settling her on the pillow, I watched for several minutes until I saw her chest move.

"Casey . . .," Eleanora said from the doorway, but I put up my hand to stop her. I didn't want to hear an apology.

I just wanted something to occupy the time till morning, and I realized that I hadn't eaten all day. There was no food in the house, but I didn't feel much like cooking anyway. And it had already become apparent that Eleanora couldn't even fry an egg. I didn't want to let her near the stove to try.

"How about if I go get us some burgers?" I said. Eleanora eyed me strangely, and I thought perhaps she hadn't heard right.

"Would you like a hamburger?" I repeated. "I'll run up to McDonald's."

"A hamburg steak?" she said. "Hmm, that might be nice. I like mine medium rare, lover."

She had an odd sense of humor.

"Fries?" I said.

"French-fried potatoes?" she said.

"Yeah." But like anyone else, she was capable of overdoing it.

"No sir. If I don't watch my girlish figure, nobody else will, either."

When I got back, Eleanora was seated in front of the television, just a few feet away, again transfixed. She had the remote in her hand (somehow we had reacquired cable without my paying a cent) and had settled on MTV. On the screen, three black women in painted-on short shorts, midriffs bare, gyrated while a male rapper walked among them, stroking his microphone.

Eleanora's mouth hung open. "Sweet mother of God," she said. "Help me, baby Jesus."

When she noticed I was in the room, she flicked the set off.

"I need me some new rags," she said.

I got two plates from the kitchen and pulled a couple of Big Macs and a large fries from the sack. Eleanora peaked under the lid of one.

"Hmm. Small," she said.

"Yeah, I think they're shrinking them. Maybe I should've gotten two for each of us."

Eleanora clutched her burger with both hands and took a bite that made half disappear. Suddenly, her eyes rolled back in her head and she moaned, low and long.

I put down my sandwich.

"You okay?"

She regained her composure, wiped a dab of sauce from her chin, and licked the fingers clean.

"What is this heavenly creation?" she said.

"It's still a Big Mac," I said, and I watched her a little more closely than usual as we both finished our dinner.

❧

At about nine that evening, I began setting up for my vigil. I carried a cushion from the sofa and a pillow from my bed to the bathroom and placed them on the floor near the shower. A look at M. P. revealed that she was still with us, breathing slowly and barely perceptibly, eyes half shut in artificial sleep. I plugged in a night light from Gin's vanity and removed the cover. It cast just enough light to read by, and it would've been the perfect time to begin a good book, but I was still unable to read. I hadn't read a thing for what seemed a long, long time. Since Virginia's car crash, to be exact. I could skim the comics, all right; nothing threatening there. But words, important words, words that composed meaningful sentences in thought-provoking paragraphs, the books in the den, the novels, textbooks, dictionaries, poetry volumes—they still scared the hell out of me. So as the hours dragged on in the tiny bathroom, I killed time by tearing off little bits of toilet paper and tossing them, balled up, toward the trash can in the corner. By midnight, the tile floor had me by about thirty points.

I heard movement in the hallway, and Eleanora appeared in the doorway, holding a glass with four fingers of bourbon in it and wearing my bathrobe. Her blatant informality didn't bother me much anymore. I should've been alarmed at the way she was insinuating herself into my life. I'd never made friends easily, and in the past year I'd driven off the few that I had. Eleanora, though, seemed to be a friend.

"May I come in?" she said, in a voice somewhere between a growl and a purr.

"Of course," I said. I started to get up. "I'm sorry. It didn't dawn on me that you might have to use this room at some point tonight."

She shook her head and held up a hand for me to stay put. Then she sat down directly across from me, against the vanity, so close our legs almost touched. The robe fell open a crack and revealed a brown knee, softly reflecting the light. I pretended not to notice. She took a sip from her drink, licked her lips, and motioned toward the box in the shower.

"How is she?"

"Dead to the world."

She put a hand to her mouth.

"Not *dead* dead," I said. "Not yet. You know what I mean."

She took another sip and offered me the glass. I said no, thanks.

"Oh, you are good," she said. "You are so damn good." She took another sip. "Who are you trying to impress, sitting stone-cold sober on a bathroom floor, tending to a sleeping cat? Me, perhaps?"

Again she had managed to push a button.

"I'd guess—and correct me if I'm wrong—but I'd guess that you've never really struggled with low self-esteem," I said.

Eleanora closed her eyes and chuckled, shaking her head from side to side.

"Oh, baby doll, the things you don't know."

We sat silent in the dim light for several minutes. We were so close as to make prolonged eye contact uncomfortable, but the one time I looked in her eyes, I looked hard, maybe too hard, because again, as she had that night in the Florida room, she appeared to be blending into the background, this time her dark hair and form melding, almost diffusing into the nooks around her where the light didn't reach. This time I couldn't blame booze.

I blinked and the illusion vanished, and across from me sat my roommate, smiling broadly.

"So, Casey, my man," she said. "Tell me why we're here right now. Tell me why you don't work. Why you sit in the dark all night and sleep all day. I'd say we have plenty of time."

Perhaps it was the time of night, or the tiny struggle for life going on just a few feet away, but I sensed that telling her would be like whispering a secret into the night—it would go no further. So I took a deep breath and prepared to reveal what I'd sworn to keep inside until the miserable end.

★   ★   ★

"First of all, I'm not sitting with a sick cat all night to impress you. But if it does, I'll take it," I said and tried to smile. Then I shook my head. "Nah, I gave up trying to impress anybody a long time ago."

Eleanora sipped from her drink, and now I wished I had one, too.

"I just don't want to screw anything else up," I said. I looked toward the shower stall where Mashed Potatoes lay curled in her box. "I've already done plenty of that."

Eleanora arched a brow, waiting for more.

Finally, because I could think of no other way to say it, I just said it.

CHAPTER 12

"I killed my wife."

Eleanora reacted to this news not by bolting from the room, as I might have expected, but by gently biting her lower lip, all the while her eyes riveted to mine.

"I doubt that, Casey," she said.

"Oh, I killed her, all right, though not in any typical way that would send me to prison. Nothing that honest. In fact, that would be a step up.

"I killed her with lies and deception and bullshit, and she died because she never suspected I was so good at such things."

Then I told Eleanora all the details. I told her how, after another stressful day at the college, I'd announced that I couldn't deal with student indifference and hostility any longer. Professional burnout was my excuse. I did not admit to Virginia, or to myself at the time, that any shortcomings in the classroom were probably my own. I had said, with puffed-up self-importance, that I needed to do something worthwhile with my life. I wanted to write a book, and I needed the time and the quiet to do it.

With hardly any hesitation—*damn her*—Gin had said that she could pick up the slack by taking on a few extra design jobs, expanding her territory beyond the ritzy confines of the Naples area. We could swing it financially, she'd said, if it was what we both truly wanted.

That first morning that I did not have to get up at six, shave, iron a shirt, and drive to the college was a liberation. I took a walk on the beach, fixed a good breakfast, watched *Sesame Street,* and drank coffee till I felt ready to begin. On the dining table in the Florida room I set out a notebook, a dictionary, and a Cross pen. I found the most comfortable chair—the one that didn't wobble— and removed the others. I sat down to begin.

Nothing happened. Not a word, not a thought. The potential story lines I had turned over in my mind for months suddenly seemed juvenile, hopelessly clichéd. I started a letter to an old friend instead and after writing two and a half pages pronounced it a decent first day's effort. Then I plopped myself on the sofa to absorb the mind-numbing repetition of CNN. It was okay, I told myself; nobody jumps right in. I needed some time to decompress. This time stretched into days, and then weeks, and when Gin arrived home at seven or eight at night, instead of her customary five-thirty, and asked how that day's writing had gone, I had to shake my head and say, "Nothing yet."

Sometime in the second month of my "sabbatical," I thought of a way I could avoid that nightly look of disappointment in Virginia's eyes. At a library book sale, I picked up a tattered copy of a novel called *The House of the Wolf,* by an obscure nineteenth-century British writer named Stanley J. Weyman. It was the fictional memoir of Anne, the Vicomte de Caylus, and his adventures in political intrigue in late seventeenth-century France. It was fast-moving and entertaining, and after reading it over the course of several afternoons, I sat down and began to rewrite it in one of my notebooks. Not to improve upon it or update it or adapt it. I simply copied it, word for word, changing nothing but the curious punctuation, eight to ten pages at a clip.

Each night I presented it to Virginia as my own.

I did not speak French or know much of French history. It was an absurd ruse, one that begged discovery, but if Virginia knew I was a fake, she said nothing. She actually seemed to enjoy each day's output as she would relax in the bath, and I would sit on the laundry hamper and read. She would look only mildly puzzled as I detailed battles between Catholics and Huguenots, complete with dates and names of dukes and kings and priests.

But we could not share the end of *The House of the Wolf*. Gin, on her way home from an extra job she had been working on Marco Island, met up with those tired Canadian tourists headed south.

★   ★   ★

The accident revealed more about me than decades of psychotherapy ever could have. I was a friend who was never much of a friend, a teacher who had little desire to teach, a writer who didn't write, and, finally, inexplicably, unforgivably, a husband, a love, a partner, a confidant, and a man who was at heart none of those things.

That was why, I told Eleanora, I could think of no good goddamned reason not to drink myself to oblivion every night or, if the elements lined up just right, to death. So far, I hadn't had the balls to choose a quicker method.

"Anything else you want to know?" I said.

Eleanora sighed and ran a hand through her thick hair. "That really doesn't tell me anything, lover."

"Say what?"

She took a sip of her drink, seeming to savor its feel on her lips, then sluiced some bourbon over her teeth before swallowing.

"My Lord, I do love this," she said. She smiled and lowered her head slightly. "Casey, lover, look. I know a thing or two about men. I know even more about women. Women something like your woman, I'd guess. She was in love—musta been—to do so right by you. And I'm betting she doesn't hold any grudges 'cause you pretended to work once upon a time when you didn't."

She stared into her glass, then touched it to her forehead.

"Honey, the real sin, far as I can see, is a life that don't amount to much," she said. "You got to care about living, baby, and to do that you got to touch living things. When you do, I swear they won't turn to ash."

She sat back against the cabinet and closed her eyes. "I coulda used such a lesson. Long time ago," she said. "But that's a lotta water over the dam."

"I don't think I understand," I said, but Eleanora was silent. As I watched her closed eyes, I wondered if she slept. I, too, suddenly felt exhausted, jet-lagged, as if I hadn't slept for days. Several times I thought I heard M. P. shift in her box, so I crawled over on my knees to take a look. She had not moved, but she had changed.

"Oh, M. P." I said. "Damn you."

Eleanora stirred as I lifted M. P. from the box. The cat's dead eyes, the open mouth, froze my spine.

"Goddammit," I said, and kicked the cabinet behind Eleanora with the sole of my foot.

Saying nothing, Eleanora took the cat from me, cradled her like an infant, and sat back down.

Then she sang, in a voice soft, low, slow,

"Why was I born? Why am I livin'?"

Expressionless, I squeezed out warm tears—both genuine and self-pitying—at her kind gesture.

"Why do I want for things I dare not hope for?
What do I hope for? I wish I knew . . ."

A twitch of M. P.'s front foot, a toe.

"I'm a poor fool, but what can I do?
Awww, baby, I was born to love you . . ."

A claw unsheathed and another and another. Pupils contracted at the light. Eleanora had stopped singing and set M. P. on the floor, where she took a few uneasy steps and curled up on the bath mat, purring like an engine.

"Jesus," I said.

Eleanora smiled and blinked at me slowly, seductively. Then she laughed and clapped a hand over her mouth.

"Who are you?" I said.

CHAPTER 13

After my confession and Mashed Potatoes' apparent resurrection, Eleanora and I hung together a lot, though we did not mention that evening again. The day after the fire, I'd discovered another of its casualties—the notes from Gin that I'd kept in a shoebox beneath the chair in Eleanora's room. From "Be back later—bye babe" to "Love you lots" to "Eat you?? When???" they were nothing but blackened scraps, and the loss felt like a punch in the stomach. But why risk tearing the fabric of the time Eleanora and I shared, such as it was? They were just ashes now, after all; they were not alive. When Eleanora wasn't looking, I quietly threw them away.

★   ★   ★

Soon our odd domesticity had settled into a pattern of cocktail hours, old movies, and Big Macs. Eleanora was nuts about Big Macs. During *five o'clocktails,* as Eleanora called them (sometimes four o'clocktails or even twelve o'clocktails, if she had her way), I'd drink light beer, and Eleanora would have bourbon or vodka or gin. The liquor cabinet soon ran dry, and I had only the beer to offer her. After her first, she scrunched up her face, closed an eye, and peered into the bottle.

"Yes?" I said.

"I'm looking for the buzz," she said. "It musta got stuck inside."

Since nearly burning down the house, Eleanora had given up cigarettes, at least in my presence. Thus, my pipe became a guilty pleasure, and when I'd smoke it, she seemed to glide into the tobacco cloud, closing her eyes and inhaling deeply.

★   ★   ★

A close second to Big Macs in the junk department was TV. Eleanora would sit mesmerized for hours, watching whatever happened to be on. This I couldn't take, so I brought home stacks of videotapes from the library, and we'd watch them until the sun came up. We saw every *Thin Man* at least twice, Nick and Nora's dog Asta making Eleanora long for a dog of her own. She cried through *Casablanca,* said Ilsa was a damned fool for wasting her life with a dud like Victor. She said there was just no understanding some women. I picked up some recent movies, too, but just once, because Eleanora would shout, "Child, close the drapes," whenever someone appeared naked onscreen. And I regretted having pointed out to her the REWIND button.

But what I remembered most about those days and nights was that we laughed, easy, real laughter, the kind that made you tingle for a while afterward. It had been a while since I'd laughed.

And the questions I had remained unasked for now.

One morning when she woke me, however—or, rather, when her singing woke me—she was not in much of a laughing mood.

"But what's the good of scheming? I know I must be dreaming . . ."
Her voice cracked.

I turned over and groaned and found M. P. asleep on my pillow. She opened her eyes and gave me a languid, two-eyed wink, the closest I'd get to a thank you.

"You've got eight left, old sport," I said, scratching behind her ear. "Unless you've used up a couple I don't know about."

Would that we all could be so extravagant with fate. I lay in bed for a while as Eleanora moved from song to song. She did not sing them in their entirety, only pieces. The standards, mainly, from "Embraceable You" to "As Time Goes By" to "On the Sunny Side of the Street."

Then she began another song, a slow, mournful song, almost a dirge. It was one I had not heard her sing before, and I got out of bed, pulled on a pair of shorts, and opened my door a crack to hear better. From there I could see into Eleanora's room. She stood staring into a large mirror on the wall, and I couldn't help but notice that she looked different than she had the night before. It was more than just a lack of makeup or lack of sleep. She looked distressed.

As I spied on her, she sang into the mirror about strange fruit on Southern trees, black bodies swaying in the breeze, corpses with bulging eyes, the smell of magnolias and burning flesh. It was a song about lynchings.

When she finished, her shoulders sagged, and she turned to look out the window.

"Good morning," I said and opened the door wider.

Without turning she said, "Did I wake you?"

"Yes, but that's all right. I usually try to be up by cocktail hour."

Eleanora faced me, the bags under her eyes worse up close.

"You okay?" I said.

"Sure, honey. I'm just a little pooped." She walked slowly to the edge of the bed—already made, or still made—and sat down heavily.

"I'm sorry I kept you up so late," I said, sitting on the bed opposite. "You look pretty ragged."

She slowly shook her head. "It's not sleep, lover. I never liked sleep much. Too close to death."

She was starting to worry me.

"Are you sick?" I said. "Do you need a doctor? I can call around and see if they'll fit you in. I can drive you."

"I think I just need to sing, sweetie," she said.

Relieved, I said, "Is that all? Then, hell, go right ahead and sing. I don't mind. I enjoy it, and as for the neighbors, well, screw 'em. I heard you just now and . . ."

"An audience," Eleanora said, sitting up straight and eyeing me. "Baby, a singer needs an audience, else she might as well be playing with herself."

I blinked.

"I suppose you're right," I finally said. "Of course. It's pretty obvious, isn't it? But I think I mentioned when you first got here that if you were looking for a cultural mecca, or even a place where people appreciated jazz, you made a wrong turn coming to Naples."

But now she was hooked. The light returned to her eyes, and she leaned forward, palms on her knees. "I know that, dollface," she said. "I'm not blind. But surely there's *something* nearby. A small club, maybe. An after-hours joint. Oh, I want to sing."

She looked theatrically toward the ceiling, smiled her toothy smile, and looked better than she had just five minutes before.

"Let me think," I said, drumming my fingers on the edge of the mattress. "There are places downtown that have pianos set up in a corner. Someone gets up and sings while people are eating . . ."

A withering look of contempt shut me up.

"Then there's always Miami," I said.

"Perfect," Eleanora said. She jumped up and rushed to me, lifting me off the bed with surprising ease and wrapping me in a snug embrace. "I knew I'd found the right man when I walked in this house."

Clutching my shoulders, she pushed me away slightly so she could look in my face. "And that little sports car of yours, ummm, honey. The queen's carriage is waiting." She hugged me again, then pushed away again.

"And it's Saturday," she said, bobbing her shoulders, dancing in place. "Soon to be Saturday night." She hugged again, then pushed me a final time.

"Tonight will be jumping," she said. She hurried down the hall to the bathroom. I didn't breathe again until I heard her slam the door.

I would have preferred sticking a pencil in my eye to driving to Miami on a Saturday night and searching for a jazz club. It was hardly my beloved Miami. Gin and I had honeymooned at the Biltmore Hotel in Coral Gables and promised to return for our tenth anniversary. Now I had no desire ever to go back. There'd be ghosts there, I thought, more demons of my own design. When Eleanora and I hit the road at about seven, I did my best to bury my anxiety.

"How do you know they'll even let you sing?" I asked Eleanora.

"All they'll have to do is hear me," she said.

*   *   *

About twenty minutes out of town, with the sun setting behind us on U.S. 41, Eleanora turned from looking out the window at the endless Glades and announced, "Biggest damn swamp I ever saw. Why doesn't somebody build something here?"

I looked at her, curiously.

"It's not allowed," I said.

"It seems to me somebody'd take this big bunch of nothing and do something with it," she said.

At the first scenic overlook I pulled off the road, shut off the engine, and turned off the lights.

"You have to take a leak?" Eleanora said.

As I opened my door, I told Eleanora to get out for a minute. I beckoned her to the front of the car where I'd climbed up on the hood and sat. I suggested she join me by patting on the metal.

"Are we gonna make out, lover?" she said with a wicked grin.

"No," I said. "Listen."

Silent at our arrival, the grass began to hum and vibrate in a rhythm that surrounded us. A bald eagle, its bold, hooked profile and fingered wings backlit by a red-orange sky, soared to the top branches of a cypress tree and settled into the remains of an abandoned nest. A pair of gators barked to each other, and an owl called from somewhere nearby. I looked over at Eleanora and saw goosebumps rise on her arms. She briskly rubbed herself and shivered. I smiled.

"So maybe I was wrong," she said.

I climbed down off the hood, and Eleanora did the same.

"Don't you need to rehearse?" I said, opening her door.

She said, "Silly white boy," and we sped off.

Just past Ochopee my back teeth were floating, and I pulled into the parking lot of a place called Uncle Joe's Cracker Bar and Pit Stop to use the men's room. A couple of guys sat on the porch drinking longneck Buds and jamming the heels of their boots into the ground.

"It's a long drive yet," I said to Eleanora. "And this is the only stop."

She shook her head and slouched low in her seat.

"Do you just want to get out and stretch your legs then?"

"Just do your damn business and get back in the car," she said, spitting out the words.

*   *   *

Back on the road, I stole glances at Eleanora, but in the dark I couldn't make out her expression. I decided to let it pass. Whatever demons troubled her were none of my business. Besides, who was I to judge?

*   *   *

I hadn't been to Miami for quite some time, and because of my genetically defective sense of direction, I didn't have a clue where we were or where to go once we hit the city limit. I flipped on the dome light and fumbled with the map as we inched along the

gauntlet of stoplights and hookers and hawkers that marked the
Tamiami Trail in West Miami. At one point a man approached my
window to sell me a stuffed fighting cock, mounted and complete
with barbed feet. I politely declined, and he moved to the car behind us, lovingly carrying his bird as if it were alive, its orange and
maroon feathers riffling in the warm breeze.

"You're going to have to help me out here," I said to Eleanora,
an edge to my voice. I'd always hated city driving, and this sudden bustle of activity around us made me nervous.

"Try to figure out where we need to go, will you?" I said,
pressing the open map on her.

Quietly and neatly she folded it up and put it on the floor.

"What the hell?" I said.

"Just head for the gut, honey," she said.

"The what?"

"The gut. You know the gut. It's right below the heart. Every
city's got one, baby. Just hit the gut."

"I wish I knew what you were saying."

"Downtown, my white knight," Eleanora said, reaching over
and grasping my leg, just above the knee. Her hand was large, her
grip solid. "I seem to recall a place called The Lyric that round
midnight ought to be jumping just fine."

So we drove east till we hit Biscayne Bay, south and got lost in
Coconut Grove, and north after we were forced by traffic onto
Interstate 95. I finally squeezed off the highway somewhere in
North Miami and drove south on Miami Avenue, hoping to God
that it would take us back to the Tamiami Trail and home. Our
mission, from my point of view, should be abandoned.

Eleanora, however, seemed to be having a fine time. Her head
swiveled from left to right and back again as she tried to take it
all in, the Metro trains gliding above us on neon rails, the steel and
cement high-rise hotels and banks, the tangle of interstates and
expressways that merged and knotted and shot off in all direc-

tions, and, always, the surging and bleating of hundreds and thousands of automobiles.

I was thinking about what an unusual woman she was, a real oddball, when the warning lights on the dash flashed on and the car conked out. I eased off the road into the litter-strewn parking lot of what was once a barbecue joint.

"That's great. Perfect," I said, pounding the wheel. Even the horn didn't work.

"Can you fix it, baby," Eleanora said, in the childlike tone of a little girl on the verge of disappointment.

I shot her a glare. "Not fucking likely."

I checked my watch—almost ten-thirty—and silently cursed the car gods for not allowing us to break down in the Everglades instead.

I pulled the hood release and grabbed a flashlight, but not knowing what I was looking at or for, I slammed the hood down, got back in the car, and sat sulking.

"I'll go find us a phone booth," Eleanora said, opening her door. "Do you have a nickel?"

"Are you nuts?" I said, grabbing her arm and pulling her back into her seat. "You can't go walking around here by yourself. There're muggers and rapists and killers out there."

I could see, with the help of a nearby traffic signal, Eleanora's smirk turn from green to yellow to angry red.

"Suit yourself," she grumbled. "We'll just sit here till morning, then."

"I'll be back in a minute," I said, sliding out and feeling glass crunch beneath my feet. "Keep the doors locked unless you see me headed back in a sprint."

I closed the door on Eleanora's hearty laughter.

I walked quickly to the nearest corner, glancing in doorways and alleys as I went. Eleanora had made me feel silly for being afraid, and perhaps she was right.

To my right, about midway down the block, was a pay phone,

its plastic cubicle broken out in chunks but its light still aglow. It stood in front of a Laundromat, bright with light but closed for the night, with accordion bars stretched the length of its facade.

To find that the phone actually worked would be a minor miracle, but I walked toward it, digging change from my jeans pocket. In a building across the street, a man and woman argued loudly over the blare of a television. A screaming baby silenced them. The whole scene reminded me of an overwrought Hogarth etching, and I wondered how come I'd never had to live on a street like this.

I lifted the receiver and the cord flopped to my side, useless, severed at the box. Pointlessly, I hung the receiver back up and rested my head against it. A roiling began in my guts at the prospect of a long evening here and, on top of everything else, I had to find a bathroom—and soon.

"Hey, mister!"

Crossing the street toward me were three young men, two of them carrying what looked like pillows wrapped in plastic. All were dressed alike, in baggy shorts and sports jerseys. One wore a green and orange Miami Hurricanes knit cap, pulled down past his ears. Another time and place, they could've been cocky freshmen in one of my English Comp classes. I nodded to them and began walking back to the car.

"Yo, man, I'm talking to you. You being rude."

I turned to face them as they stepped up on the curb.

"What's up?" I said. My heart beat faster.

"We got a deal for you," the one with the cap said. He held out what he carried. Up close I could see it was the cushioned top of a stool.

"Wanna buy a bar seat?" he said. "Cheap."

"Thanks just the same," I said, "but I don't have a bar." I turned to leave and one of the men put up an arm to stop me.

"You really want these seats, man," said the other one carrying a cushion.

Feigning great interest now, I examined the stool tops. "How much?" I asked Knit Cap.

"How much you got?"

Adrenaline flushed, making me sweat. Keeping my voice steady took effort.

"You a doctor?" said the guy who had stopped me from leaving.

I smiled nervously. "Do I look like a doctor?"

"You a lawyer?" he then said.

Stupidly, "Do I look like a lawyer?"

"Come on, man," said Knit Cap. "I'm tired of carrying this thing." He pushed the cushion toward me, thumping me in the chest.

"Ten bucks apiece?" I said. The voice I heard did not sound like my own. Knit Cap shook his head from side to side, while another laughed and said, "Shit."

"Your billfold, man," Knit Cap said, holding out his hand. From a pocket of the guy without a cushion came a pistol, small and terrifying in its ugliness.

"Okay," I said, "okay." My guts were white hot and sluicing, and I thought I might pass out.

"Now, motherfucker," said Knit Cap, throwing aside the stool top.

Unable to see anything but the gun, I reached, marionette-like, to my back pocket and fumbled for my wallet. In handing it over, my fingers went stiff and I dropped it on the sidewalk.

"Pick it up," said the one with the pistol, but my knees wouldn't bend.

"You better do it," said Knit Cap, moving so close to me that I could smell his stale-sweet breath. He stood almost on my foot.

"I can't," I said. "Just take it. Enjoy."

I didn't notice as one of them slipped around my side, and when his fist struck bone beside my ear, I fell to my knees as much from shock as from the force of the blow.

Through eyes swimming in reflex tears, I could see Knit Cap standing with his foot on my wallet. The three talked loudly now, all at once, but I couldn't make out the words. I seemed to be deaf in one ear. Then the voices turned to hoots and whistles, and I knew we had company.

"Hello, fellas, how's tricks?" It was Eleanora. She moved to my side and put her hand on my head.

"You all right, Casey?"

"Get back in the car, please," I said. Though I was still scared witless, my voice no longer shook.

"It's boring back there, lover. Don't make me go back."

"Do it for me. Please."

"Bitch and him a couple," said Knit Cap, whose voice had seared itself into my brain. This was greeted by more hoots and cackling laughter.

"Beg pardon?" said Eleanora. She had removed her hand from my head and moved closer to the trio.

"Don't," I heard myself say.

"Bitch, what you sayin' 'Beg pardon'?" said Knit Cap. "I'll smack your nigger face."

"Does your momma know you talk like that?" Eleanora said.

I made a move to get up, but a gun barrel stabbed my cheek, and I sat down on the pavement.

"From now on you can refer to me as 'Lady,'" Eleanora went on, to a chorus of jeers and loud insults. I wanted to close my eyes, make it all go away.

"I have a little something I think might interest you boys," said Eleanora, stepping still closer to Knit Cap. Slowly and coolly she lifted the hem of her skirt, exposing one sturdy leg to the top of her stockings. The eyes of the three widened, and Knit Cap, almost slobbering, said, "Bitch is in heat."

What happened next was an illusionist's sleight-of-hand and a blur of commotion. Knit Cap had reached for Eleanora's breast as she brought her hand from the stocking top toward his face and gently traced a line from his temple to his top lip. He smiled quizzically a split second before the left side of his face opened up in a veil of bright red blood.

"Shit!" he screamed, covering his face with his hands. "Bitch cut me!" He stepped backward, turned, and stumbled toward a storefront, where he tried to examine himself in the window. Hyperventilating, he spewed blood on the glass with each breath.

The guy still holding a stool top moved toward him as if to help, thought better of it, and instead sprinted down the sidewalk and out of sight, cushion tucked tightly under his arm.

That left only the one with the pistol, and Eleanora said, "C'mere, baby doll," and beckoned him with her pinkie.

"I don't need this bullshit," he said, stuffed the gun in his pocket, and strolled nonchalantly across the street.

I stood up, dazed and staring at the unfortunate figure who stood dazed and staring at himself in a shop window. His cap, no longer orange and green but dark red, he pressed without success against his wound.

I might have stood there till morning had Eleanora not grabbed my hand and jerked me toward the car.

"We don't need to meet Junior's big brother," she said as she scooped up my wallet and we hurried along the sidewalk. We got in the car quickly and locked the doors.

Back to reality, I moaned at our prospects. "The car won't start," I said.

"Try it now," Eleanora said. It fired up easily.

"Put your seatbelt on," I scolded. I glanced over my left shoulder and squealed tires leaving the curb. Eleanora put a hand on the wheel.

"What?" I said.

"Baby, I think you found the gut."

CHAPTER 14

I didn't regain my composure until we were headed west, city lights receding behind us, the Alligator Alley tollbooth glowing faintly about a half mile ahead, then nothing but a sea of dark grasses and stars. I finally looked over at Eleanora and was about to say what a rush that whole episode had been, and that she was great, and wouldn't it be good to get home, and on and on.

Her expression stopped me dead. Melancholy had a face, and it was hers. And I knew the reason. I was partly to blame.

Yards from the tollgate I pulled the car out of line and off the road.

"We'll find you a place to sing," I said. "I don't know where, and it won't be tonight, but we'll do it. I promise."

She looked at me, then smiled slowly, her cheeks growing fatter, her teeth gleaming in the dashboard light.

"I think you'll be surprised and proud of me, too," she said.

And my heart damn near broke.

★　　★　　★

The drive back across the Everglades was, thankfully, uneventful. Eleanora slept most of the way, and I was so tired I had no energy left for worrying. A mechanical breakdown now would be small potatoes indeed, a mere blip on the hassle meter.

I was glad that Eleanora slept because it gave me a chance, in the quiet and dark, to bring back Virginia. I had been doing this for months, re-creating in increasing detail vignettes, scenes, whole days of our life together. I imagined it was something prisoners might do to preserve their sanity. At first bad memories would intrude: the times we shouted at each other, or when she would follow me out of the house and down the driveway when all I wanted was a break from it all. Those thoughts I did not fight. I figured they were just defensive, meant to force my brain to let go, to move on, but of course I couldn't. Finally, the best memories returned, and when they did, it was with a vengeance. Often, out by the pool at night, snuggled in a comfortable beer buzz, I would dream awake for hours, reliving a scene so completely that I was startled when I finally went inside and did not find Virginia making toast or sitting up in bed, sipping a mug of hot tea and reading a book.

This night, as I drove through the swamp, an ass-whupping black jazz singer in Virginia's seat, I went back to our trip to New York the year before Gin and I married. At the time she was already living in Naples, looking for a job, and I was finishing a teaching stint in Tallahassee, so we were to meet up at the Atlanta airport. Gin looked small and radiant as she strode confidently through the concourse in the new trench coat she had bought for the trip. I tried to hide as she looked around for me, and when I saw the first sign of concern on her face as she checked her watch, I sneaked up behind her, wrapping her bundled body in a bear hug and burying my face in her hair.

"Jack," she said, goofing on me, "I told you I was meeting my fiancé here."

I bit her neck.

It was Gin's first trip to New York, and we did it right, getting a room we could scarcely afford at the Marriott Marquis, one near the top with a picture window that overlooked Times

Square. It was the holiday season, and snow and decorations softened the city's ugly corners. It was the first snowfall either of us
had seen since we were kids, and from twenty-seven stories up,
our view was an elaborate Christmas tableau.

Though we had been traveling and awake all night, we
were too excited to rest, and we wrapped ourselves up and set
off on a long walk, eventually ending up in Central Park. It
was bitter cold with stinging wind gusts, but we didn't much
care. The freezing weather invigorated our Florida blood and
made it so we had the park to ourselves. Delighted, we
crunched through snowbanks and sipped hot chocolate from
the park's luncheonette.

When the cold finally became unbearable, we left the park and
hurried across Park Avenue, ducking into the tiny upscale shops
and feigning interest in India cotton gowns and jewel-handled
daggers, all the while giggling like kids skipping class. When the
merchants' hoverings and solicitations became too much, we set
off again, huddled together, Gin's bare hand in my overcoat pocket, clutching mine. This Florida girl had forgotten to bring gloves,
so we shared my pair.

We got back to our room early evening and shucked our
coats, sweaters, and scarves. I went down to the lobby to buy a
bottle of wine. When I returned, the lights in the room were off,
making the view more spectacular.

"Well?" Gin said coyly, standing by the drapes.

"It's a fantastic view, isn't it?" I said. "I'm glad we did this."

"Anything else?" she said, glancing repeatedly at the window.

"I notice you're not wearing a slinky nightgown."

She cleared her throat and motioned with her head toward the
window. As my eyes grew accustomed to the dark I grinned
hugely because I had not seen it immediately, it blended so well
with the multicolored lights outside. Gin had erected a tiny
Christmas tree, complete with lights and little glass balls, on the

table before the window. She had carried it all the way from Florida.

Then, from behind her back, she produced the tiny recorder she'd used in college to tape lectures and pressed PLAY. Out of it came the voice of Billie Holiday, small and distant but clear and lovely:

> *Ask the sky above,*
> *And ask the earth below*
> *Why I'm so in love*
> *And why I love you so.*
> *Couldn't tell you, though I'd try dear,*
> *Just why I'm yours . . .*
> *When you went away*
> *You left a glowing spark.*
> *Trying to be gay is whistlin' in the dark.*
> *I am only what you make me—*
> *Come take me—*
> *I'm yours.*

We both knew it was corny, but Keats was right: A thing of beauty is a joy forever. And that day, that evening, that precise moment when Virginia and I swapped souls completely—in the company of Lady Day—well, it'll stay with me till I die.

Shortly after the trip I realized that the reasons I had remained single no longer seemed important. Early the following spring, again huddled with Virginia against the cold, this time at a Florida State baseball game in Tallahassee, I asked her if she would marry me.

CHAPTER 15

When we got back home, Eleanora and I retired to our rooms, irritable and arguing over who was more beat. I checked on Mashed Potatoes, who lay curled on my bed, her head on my pillow. If she had moved a whisker since I'd last seen her almost twelve hours earlier, I couldn't tell. I took off my shoes and collapsed next to her.

When I woke, the sun was shining and the house was quiet. I stared at the ceiling fan, really focused on it, to make sure I was home and safe in my own bed. Yet something gnawed at me, a feeling that the previous evening's events were unresolved. With rising anxiety I recalled the near mugging, the cold pistol barrel stuck in my face, the vicious slashing by Eleanora. I got out of bed quickly, ran to the bathroom, and flipped up the lid of the toilet. I kneeled before it, nauseated, but couldn't vomit. I stuck a finger down my throat, with no success, and sat down on the cool tile.

★   ★   ★

I showered, toweled off, pulled on a T-shirt and some shorts. Without checking, I already knew that, for whatever reason, Eleanora had gone. I didn't check her room; there was no need. There is a palpable feeling to an empty house, one I had become intimate with. But she would be back; I knew it.

I decided on a long beach walk and fed M. P. before going out to the car. Next door, Jason Foster was throwing a baseball high in the air, staggering under it before making the catch, then acknowledging the adulation of an invisible crowd, doffing his Braves cap.

"Hello," I called, and waved.

He stopped dead, his eyes wide, then bolted for his house, the screen door slamming behind him.

"Mom, that man next door . . ." I heard him holler, and then his voice trailed off as he galloped through the house.

Across the street, the elderly lady plucked weeds from her lawn, her daily ritual. She had looked up when Jason shouted.

"Good morning," I called, and waved. She nodded just once, then pulled her sunbonnet tighter on her head and returned to her weeding, turning her back to me.

I had suspected it for some time, but now it seemed confirmed—I was the neighborhood screwball. I drove to Lowdermilk Park, walked the two miles to Doctor's Pass, climbed the rocks, and sat for a long time watching the pleasure boats stream out into the Gulf.

With Eleanora gone, I tried hard not to return to my old habits, but the lure was irresistible. So once again I spent nights by the pool or lying on the living room floor with M. P. and listening to jazz. I played a lot of Billie Holiday, even buying several more CDs, a foolish extravagance considering my financial situation. I studied the liner notes and pictures that accompanied the discs, and I listened closely to the music, letting it float into my waking dreams. I noted how Billie's voice and style changed dramatically from the youthful confidence and exuberance of her early stuff to her final recordings, during which she seemed to get through songs of memory and regret through sheer force of will. And as her voice changed, so did her appearance. Drastically. Early in her career, her photos showed a smooth-skinned beauty, eyes large and dark and soulful, just like Eleanora.

At the end, a short ten years later, Billie looked like the grandmother of her earlier self, her face completely changed, skin pitted, cheeks sagging, eyes swollen. As I studied and listened and drifted and dreamed, I sensed that her decline was more than the result of hard living—it was the product of profound disappointment, in the world she lived in and, more than anything, in herself. I thought I knew what she felt, and though I have always been a skeptic, I closed my eyes and in my own clumsy way prayed for her soul. And for my own.

God bless you, Eleanora.

And in the solitude and quiet, I finally let this crazy reality take shape: Billie Holiday was living in my house. Denying it any longer seemed absurd, and even though I accepted it, I certainly couldn't explain it. I had ten thousand questions and more, as would anyone who had a ghost sashay into his life, but they'd probably never be asked. Besides, I already knew the answer to the most important one; Eleanora's purpose here was obvious. She would help me go where I belonged, where I'd been wanting to go ever since Virginia's accident.

Shortly after Gin died, I broke all the windows in our bedroom, then took myself to a psychiatrist to learn that I was suffering from clinical depression. As if by putting a name to the problem we could immediately set about fixing it. I didn't tell the doctor about my phony writing life, or perhaps we could have amended the label to "clinical guilt" or "terminal worminess."

The shrink told me that I could begin to pull myself out of it by engaging in some sort of worthwhile work, something that would help other people. Besides, he added, the bills don't stop coming just because you're feeling bad. I asked him if he was referring to *his* bill, and when he didn't answer, I asked what sort of worthwhile work he thought I could find in Naples. Perhaps serving lobster and rice pilaf to retired industrialists at Bear's Paw Country Club?

"It's perfectly natural to feel animosity toward your surroundings at a time like this," he said.

"Screw you," I said.

We compromised. I would do the things that I used to find enjoyable. And, the doctor advised, don't shy away from things that Gin and I used to do together. I had to learn to go it alone now.

So I went back to the informal gatherings of the Gulf Coast Gonzo Sailors, a ragtag group of sailing bums and men and women who occasionally rented Sunfish at the beach. We would meet at a smoky faux English pub in the warehouse district and talk about whatever might be of interest that day. Rarely would we discuss sailing.

When I had first moved to Naples, this is what passed as my social life, my guys' night out, and while I never considered any of the members close friends, they were pleasant company. Gin had only gone with me once, so I figured going without her now would be bearable.

On the doctor's advice, I also began taking adult education classes again, brushing up on my Spanish, trying to learn German and French. I would even trade bad jokes and talk baseball with the old guys in the class, just as I had always done. But something was different. I had what I can only describe as a reality problem. I would be at the pub, or crewing on someone's boat, or struggling to conjugate French verbs, and yet I would not be there. It was as if I were visiting someone else's dream or had stepped into a scene from another man's life and didn't have the script. That other man, of course, had been me. So to kill that bastard off, once and for all, I stopped doing anything I had ever done before.

CHAPTER 16

I returned home early one morning from my monthly shopping excursion to restock the larder with tuna, mayonnaise, bananas, oranges, black beans, rice, and cat chow—subsistence food for the household. It was past dawn but still misty, and as I pulled into the driveway, I stopped abruptly. Perched atop the porch swing I had bought Virginia for our last anniversary was an owl. It was so large, at first I thought it was a possum or raccoon. The rare sight made me smile and, not wanting to disturb it, I sat in the car for a long time, watching. Then it occurred to me why the owl was there. Four blocks away, Coastland Center Mall, already the region's largest, was undergoing a major expansion, clearing acres of pines and scrub to build a parking garage. The owl was now without a home.

The gaze it fixed on me suddenly made me shudder, and I quickly hauled the groceries inside, slamming the front door.

*   *   *

As I passed the telephone nook, I noticed a blinking light. I had a message. I tossed the grocery bags at the kitchen counter, missing with one whose contents then slipped out item by item, hitting the floor. I wanted it to be Eleanora, ignoring the obvious notion that it would be exceedingly odd for her to start a game of phone tag.

It was instead a man's voice, and in my disappointment I punched the machine off, went into the kitchen, and threw groceries into cabinets. Only later did I stand cans and bottles and boxes upright and clean up what had broken. Then I sat down next to the phone and replayed the message.

"Casey," the voice said, the inflection rolling like a marble along a table, then dropping off the edge. Slow, Southern, erudite, ancient. "I just wanted to warn you that we might once again be neighbors, for a couple of months, at least. It's a long story, but it involves the death of my dear old mother, a monstrosity she owned on the beach, and a bevy of cockatiels, if that's how cockatiels elect to gather. I will call you when I get there, but let me give you the number regardless."

I heard a fumbling on the other end, then what sounded like the receiver plunging into a tub of water.

"Casey, are you there?" the voice said. "My poor boy, have I drowned you? You see, I must bathe in Epsom salts three times a day, and it's difficult as hell to do two things at once when you're old as dirt, and I had that number right here by the tub . . ." (more splashing and loud sloshing, a bump, a muffled "*Son of a Virgin, my ass . . .,*" and the message resumed).

"Here it is." He gave me the number and that was that. I didn't write it down.

★   ★   ★

To try to take my mind off Eleanora, I recalled everything I could about Goodman Hardin.

When I was at Florida State, he had lived on the other side of a stone wall that divided my place from his. My place was the left half of a tumbledown duplex; his was one of the last great Tallahassee homesteads, in the Hardin family for generations and not yet gobbled up by the voracious campus. I'd lived next to him for several semesters before I ever saw him, and our first meeting I would like to forget.

The semester had just ended, and a buddy and I were celebrating with a case of cheap beer. With a sudden hankering for fireworks, we decided to smash the empties, and my neighbor's rough stone-and-mortar wall was the perfect palette.

Bottle after bottle exploded against the rocks that—I later learned—Goodman himself had assembled and placed forty-odd years before. Cackling like idiots and congratulating ourselves, we hadn't noticed the man now standing with us, holding a beer bottle as if examining it. He was middle-aged, taller than either of us, and wearing a white undershirt with a tweed sportcoat to stave off the chill. His hair was neatly combed, and I remembered thinking, even drunk, that he'd surely been in bed and we'd awakened him, but he'd taken the time to make himself presentable before confronting the creeps vandalizing his property.

"If you are going to use my wall for your merriment," he said, "then couldn't you throw a full one over it now and again so that I might enjoy your little prank myself?"

He could not have shamed us more if he'd called our mothers. I looked at the ground, pawed it with my toe.

"I'm Goodman Hardin," he said, extending his hand. "I guess we're neighbors. How do you do, *neighbor?*" His tone was thick and sweet as sorghum.

"I'm sorry," I said, unable to look him in the eyes.

"I'll bet you are." He gestured toward the wall. "Because if you'll notice, all of the broken glass is on your side, and I know for a fact that you are not going to feel like cleaning it up later this morning. But you'll have to anyway."

He then turned and walked away, disappearing around the corner and into the quiet dark.

At dawn, before picking up every last chunk and shard, I went over to Goodman's place to give him a sober apology. We were fast friends for the rest of my time in Tallahassee.

★   ★   ★

But I hadn't seen him in nearly fifteen years and didn't know how or why he'd looked me up. Now, his sudden intrusion into my (somewhat) ordered life was a complication I could do without. So I would treat him as I had treated all my friends since the accident: If I ignored him, he, too, would undoubtedly go away.

*   *   *

Two days later he left another message, and, like it or not, Goodman Hardin was now back in my life.

Never driving a car or even knowing how to was just one of his peculiarities. He'd never worked at a job in the time I knew him—he didn't need to—though some at the university remembered him as a professor of comparative religion or perhaps Romantic poetry. As a teen, he once told me, he had gone from New England prep-school student to Golden Gloves champ because the kids back in Florida had questioned his sexual preferences. He never married, never had a lover of either sex that he let me know about. And he once met Virginia when he invited us to his sailboat on the Panhandle coast, where we sat tied to the dock, never hoisting a sail, he and I getting looped—he on aquavit and I on beer—while Virginia told ridiculous stories about the Flying Dutchman and sailors lost at sea. When Gin left to use the facilities on the pier, Goodman leaned close to me, clinked his oddly shaped bottle against my beer bottle, and said, "She's a good one, boy. Don't you let go of her."

After two unreturned phone calls, surely my old friend would get the message. For now I had more immediate concerns. I was going to find Eleanora.

*   *   *

The irony of this search was not lost on me: Most people visited by spirits did their damnedest to get rid of them. I wanted mine back. I was eager to get on with it, or perhaps there was something else pulling me.

I checked the wine bars and white-bread jazz clubs downtown. I popped into the cigar bars and what looked to be pick-up spots. It had been so long since I'd been out and around the town that I was amazed at the hip, trendy, loud, gaudy, neon, steel transformation of the place. Transmogrified into restaurants/cafés/apartments were the old mom-and-pop joints selling coconuts carved into monkey faces and seashell Christmas trees. Eleanora would not be here, I thought.

I bought sacks of Big Macs and stacked them in the refrigerator until the whole house smelled of onions and pickles. I tried to re-create whatever I had done to conjure her in the first place, playing her CDs nearly nonstop (Jesus, the sensation was strange), but nothing.

In desperation I checked the booths at McDonald's, counted canoes at the Conservancy, looked for her at the mall.

And I missed her.

CHAPTER 17

Late at night the walls pressed in like they never had before, so I'd drive to the beach and slip my car into the driveway of some ungated beachfront mansion, coasting to a darkened part of the lot and quietly getting out. I'd remove my shoes as soon as I hit the sand and walk for a mile or so, looking down at the phosphorescent organisms in the surf or up at the bright pinholes in the sky. When my ankles would ache from the sand, I'd find a dry spot that no condo floodlights reached, dig myself a little seat amid the hanging tangle of sea grape branches, and stare out at the enormous and terrifying black Gulf.

★ ★ ★

One night, when the moon was almost full, I had company. Five people—two sturdily built men, what looked to be a middle-aged woman, a stooped older woman draped in a shawl, and a slim young girl—walked quickly past my spot in the sand, whispering to each other in Spanish. My eyes accustomed to the dark, I could see them, but they were unaware of me and focused on something at sea. They stopped about thirty yards away on a darkened stretch of beach. The men helped the older woman to the sand, and the rest walked to the water's edge. A narrow beam of light shot from the hand of one of the men and was soon lost on the waves. Quickly he extinguished it. He did this many more times over the next few hours until finally, lifting the old woman from the sand, they trooped slowly past me, still not seeing me as I sat motionless in the low bower of branches. The young girl came so close that she kicked sand on my leg, giving me, momentarily, the heady sensation of being invisible.

The next two nights this scene was replayed in nearly exact detail, with one minor change. Now, when they left the beach, the old woman was crying.

The fourth night, the moon's brightest, I again sat in the sand, again hidden, expecting them. I had grown attached to them, though they were oblivious to me, and I wanted to see their surreal drama play itself out.

This night, when the man flashed his light, it was met by another flash offshore. The young girl whooped, and the middle-aged woman put her arm around her and pulled her head close to silence her. The man onshore flashed his light again. It was mirrored out in the Gulf, this time closer. Then the lights stopped, and all of us peered out at the water. Finally, a shape appeared. It looked like a floating sleeper sofa with a loose sheet flying free. The two men onshore, and the girl, waded into the surf, the girl getting in too deep and losing her footing. All three pulled at the craft, struggling to bring it to shore. When it beached, several shapes staggered off, and I saw one of the men reach into the boat and pull out a bundle. Two people from the craft, a man and a woman, collapsed on the sand. The man was handed a bottle, and he handed it to the woman, who drank deeply. The bundle was passed to the old woman, and the others helped the two to their feet. Three more children then climbed out of the boat and were hugged by those onshore.

The group turned and walked back toward the road, the children needing some support, and I soon noticed that they were headed not just in my direction but right at me, perhaps to disappear into the trees. I thought of jumping up to let them know I was there, but it was already too late. Just as the young girl was about to trip over me, she stopped short and let out a scream. The old woman cried, "Dios mío," and the infant she held began to wail. All heads turned to me, but no one spoke.

A long moment passed before one of the men leaned toward me and whispered, pleadingly, "No policía, por favor."

"No policía," I said, shaking my head. I got up and followed, several feet behind them. When we reached the street, I hurried to my car and pulled an old beach blanket from the backseat, shaking the sand from it. I caught up to them and handed it to one of the women. I asked in college Spanish if they knew where the hospital was, and several nodded. But I could tell by the looks on their faces that the hospital was the last place they would go.

I couldn't sleep when I got home, and I paced the house compulsively, drinking way too much coffee and sucking on my pipe until I gagged. I replayed the beach scene over and over in my mind, and each time the hairs on the back of my neck bristled. At the very least, it had been one remarkable job of sailing, to take that tattered craft from the surf off Cuba to a pinpoint beach landing almost two hundred miles away. But that wasn't what awed me. These people, the ones on the beach and those who stumbled from the homemade boat, possessed something that I lacked, something that I probably never had, and I would have given everything I owned to trade places with any one of them.

★   ★   ★

The landing had occurred too late to make the morning papers, but I knew at first light some condo watchdog, sipping coffee and reading *The Wall Street Journal,* would spy the contraption and call the cops. So at 7:00 A.M. I turned on the local news. Sure enough, it was the lead story.

"The refugee invasion has touched the pristine shores of Southwest Florida," the newscaster intoned. They had a camera on the scene, and it slowly panned the little boat. Its design was rougher even than I had imagined. Planks and inner tubes were fastened together with what looked like shoelaces and strips of bedding. The tiller was a crowbar, with a chunk of plywood as a rudder.

What followed the footage was a call-in segment during which concerned, sometimes panicked, citizens demanded local authorities to protect them. The announcer finally ended the piece by saying that anyone who witnessed the illegal landing should call the police, marine patrol, or FBI immediately.

I clicked off the television and headed for the beach.

I walked the shore for miles, toward downtown and past and, after a moment's hesitation, to Seventh Avenue South and the house where Goodman Hardin was staying.

I scraped through a sea grape hedge into the large overgrown back lot. The house in the distance was a sprawling thing, pink and gray with green accents, courtesy of a particularly vigorous strain of mold. Gutters and downspouts lay on the ground, and missing shingles made a patchwork of the roof. It looked uninhabited, maybe uninhabitable.

*   *   *

I stood there for a long time, the sand still morning-cool, the far-off shout of a child hustling from a wavelet the only sound of life. To go up to the house would mean involvement, involvement meant entanglement and obligation, and those didn't play out too well for me. I walked away and walked back and walked down the beach and returned. I would tell Goodman what I'd seen that morning, because he would understand.

*   *   *

At the back porch I rapped on the door frame.

"Hello?" I called. The door to the rest of the house was open, but inside it was dark. Then a figure, tall, gaunt, appeared in the doorway and emerged into the sunlight.

"Casey, boy," said my old neighbor. "A delightful surprise."

He opened the screen door and pumped my hand, and I tried to take it all in. Though still taller than I, Goodman was now quite thin. There was less of him in other ways as well. The top half of his left ear was gone, as was the tip of his nose. Brown spots mottled his face and arms, and a deep indentation above his right eye indicated surgery there as well. I could only think that the years he'd spent tending his garden, sailing his boat, and walking everywhere, all in the merciless Florida sun, had finally caught up with him and were now eating him alive. He looked like a deteriorating old sepia print.

And then I noticed the cockatiel on his shoulder, noticed the screen porch was filled with cockatiels, maybe a dozen of them, bobbing, staring, turning sideways to look at us.

"This is Bother," Goodman said, motioning toward the one perched near his partial ear. I reached up to stroke its breast and it latched its beak on me, hard.

"Ow, son of a . . ."

"That's why he's Bother," Goodman said. "They're all Bother. I don't know their real names, not that I much care. It seems I have inherited them from Mother's caretaker. He saw fit to die shortly after she did, and by a process of elimination, they have become this white man's burden."

His voice was still strong, slow, drippingly Southern. It was a voice I had always enjoyed.

"You own this place?" I said. It had to be worth millions.

"So I've been told. I am just having some coffee. Please say you'll join me, my boy. It's been too long."

I said I would.

We talked little about what had happened in the intervening

fifteen years, though he knew I'd gotten married, didn't know Gin had died. When I hadn't responded to his phone calls, he'd assumed I was too busy with family and career to be bothered with an eccentric old man.

We talked about that morning's raft landing, and the old sailor's eyes widened in appreciation when he contemplated the skill that had gotten the refugees safely to this shore.

He walked me around the house—it was labyrinthine, built in the thirties, with a "gathering room," as Goodman called it, mirrored on all sides and big enough to spiral a football in. It was a tacky place, Goodman admitted, as his mother was a dear but tacky woman. He had given away almost all of the furniture, keeping only a chair, a reading lamp, a table and chairs, a bed, and a few other items he shoved into closets or unused rooms. It was all the furniture a man should decently own, he said, and certainly all he needed as he decided what to do with the old place.

He had quit drinking on doctor's orders (he said he could tell by looking that I had not), and he'd even given up his beloved panatelas. The only pleasures left to him here were reading the Romantics and taking long, slow swims in the Gulf, in defiance of the sun.

I told him that my joys for a while had been limited to alcohol, tobacco, and jazz, preferably all at the same time. I did not, of course, mention Eleanora.

When I left he invited me to return soon. I said I'd come, and, surprising myself, I thought I might. After all, Goodman seemed to need a friend.

CHAPTER 18

When I was trying to pull off my writing ruse, I assuaged my guilt somewhat by directing creative energies elsewhere—into cooking. I became a tireless experimenter with international cuisines, and Gin and I traveled the world without leaving the bungalow.

Preparations began with shopping in the late morning, hitting the supermarket for staples (scallions and fresh ginger; tomatoes and red peppers; zucchini and spinach; allspice and cumin and oranges; yellow rice, chicken, and shellfish for steaming skillets of paella), and then searching the small ethnic markets—some far outside of town—for rarer spices and herbs, fruits and vegetables. Fresh jackfruit, aromatic, sweet, and as long as my arm, hung outside Yu Hang's. Sir Jerome's Caribbean Market offered mountains of Scotch bonnets, the flame of Jamaican jerk. Anna Maria's sold arugula, Anna herself insisting it was essential for any salad. Fresh grouper I got right from the docks, and, perhaps most satisfying of all, mangoes for chutney and ice cream, and avocados for guacamole, I plucked from our jungled backyard.

The preparation would take hours, the eating less than thirty minutes. Still, the payoff seemed worth it.

★   ★   ★

One evening after feasting, while Gin and I rinsed dishes in the sink, she said, casually, "You know, a dinner like that deserves a special dessert."

"Okay, what would you like?" I said, still focused on cleaning up the kitchen. When I looked up again, she stood in the doorway, naked, her neck and chest flushing gorgeously.

"Let's go for a ride," she said. My car keys dangled from her fingertips, rested against her thigh.

It took a moment for the notion to sink in.

"No robes?" I said.

"No towels, no shoes, no hats or gloves. Just the keys we need to go." She laughed. "Whatsa matter? Chicken?"

"Ha!" I said, and stripped, my heart thudding as my briefs hit the floor. I wondered which of us would call it off first. I turned out the light and opened the door quietly, as if we were escaping. The night was cool and blessedly moonless, and as I pulled the door closed behind us and locked it, my body tingled so thoroughly that I shivered from head to toe.

I opened the car door for Gin, and she leaned into the backseat, the pale skin of her buttocks catching what little light the stars offered. Out of the car flew beach towels, a sun shield, a cloth I used to check the oil. Nothing whatever remained to cover ourselves with should the car break down or, worse, we get stopped by the cops.

Gin looked at me and smiled nervously. I could barely see her eyes.

She slipped into the front seat, and I joined her on my side, thrilling at each new sensation—the coolness and stickiness of the vinyl, the errant grains of sand and raised threads on the seat, the way the pedals seemed overpowering against my bare feet. Every nerve ending danced.

"So where to, my love?" I said.

"Do I have to think of everything?" she said, looking silly and vulnerable and small, so close I could smell her musk. I slipped in a tape and turned it low as Billie Holiday sang of winter in Vermont.

"It's not too late to back out," I said.

"Hmmmph," she said.

I drove to the beach, a trip of little more than a mile that now seemed indefinitely longer. We got stuck at a light on U.S. 41, trucks and SUVs sitting tall all around us, and I couldn't bring myself to look to see if we were being watched. Gin's fingernails bit into my thigh.

We parked quickly and dashed for the surf, plunging in while laughing like idiots. The water, shockingly cold, made us both holler. By now we were out of breath.

"Let's remember that we did this when we grow old and boring," Gin said. "And tell our daughter about it, though of course we'll forbid her ever to do the same."

I pulled her to me and she wrapped her legs around me, settling herself in a perfect position. One hand on my shoulder, she reached down with the other and guided me in with surprising ease. Then while holding each other tightly, hearing around us the soft splashes of tiny fish trying to escape bigger fish, we let the waves rock us to orgasm.

When we emerged from the surf, freezing, we warmed each other with friction from palms and fingers and ran back to the car, embarrassed and delighted.

The loop of that scene, when it plays in my brain, is one of the most painful of all.

CHAPTER 19

I did pay Goodman another visit. The following day. I again approached from the beach—it seemed the only real access to the
place—and knocked on the screen door. A chorus of cockatiels
squawked painfully.

"Enter," I heard Goodman call from somewhere inside. I
poked my head into the gathering room, the mirrors creating a
dizzying illusion of four or five Goodman Hardins standing on
the same number of ladders, trying to hang four or five big sacks
of something from the rafters.

"You're just in time," he said. "Give this bag a boost from the
bottom, won't you? I need it to reach this hook."

"There," he said, descending, folding up the ladder, and standing it in a corner of the cavernous room. He looked up to ad-
mire his handiwork. It was a heavy bag, the type you see in
boxing gyms.

I stepped back, folded my arms, and nodded.

"It makes the room," I said. "It's the one piece that was missing. Wherever did you find it?"

"It's for removing anger," he said, ignoring me, giving the bag
a push that sent it swinging into me.

I was puzzled by the curious choice of words.

He said, "It's for you, my boy. Take a lick and see for yourself how cathartic it is."

"For me? I'm not angry. Christ."

He grinned like a goon, and I could see there was no way past this moment without my at least striking the thing. So I took an embarrassed swing and connected (it would've been hard to miss), barely rocking the sack. The canvas scraped my knuckles, making them bleed, and now I was angry.

"Casey, Casey, Casey," Goodman said. "A pathetic display of manhood." He moved around the bag himself, striking it from different sides, setting it in crazy motion. I was startled at how solidly the old guy popped it. Yet he moved with a lightness, de-liberateness, and grace—picture Baryshnikov in Hamlet's fight scene. And for a just a second I could see him as a young Golden Gloves champ, proud and prep-school polite, more than a half century before. Cockatiels skittered past the open door, fright-ened by the unaccustomed commotion.

"But you are not a lost cause," Goodman said, getting winded now. He stopped and steadied the bag. "All you need is some in-struction."

I slowly shook my head. "Thanks just the same, but I don't think so."

He wrapped a mottled arm around my shoulders and said, "Lord Byron boxed. Did you know that?"

I did.

"And I'll let you in on a little secret: I am Lord Byron."

Crazy old fool.

"Besides, what else have you got to do?"

★　　★　　★

He had me there. And the fifty push-ups and hundred sit-ups he asked me to do each morning, and the daily running on the beach ("So the bag won't get the best of you, boy. Now that would be humiliating."), well, they'd do me no harm, I supposed.

I would let Goodman Hardin teach me to box so that I could raise a sweat each afternoon in his rambling, crumbling mansion by the sea, to the shrieks of cockatiels (Where was their anger release?), and I would learn enough to beat holy hell out of a big bag full of sand and in the process make myself less angry.

It made perfect sense to me.

"Let me see your stance," Goodman said the morning of our first lesson. Paddle fans twisted lethargically overhead as we stood in the mirrored great room. Self-conscious, I assumed a pose that I had last employed on a playground in St. Louis when Mark Devereau called me Pooper Cooper for about the six-hundredth time. I had my limits.

Goodman stepped toward me, reached out, and gently pushed my left shoulder. I rocked backward and had to take a step to regain my balance.

"That'll never do, Casey, lad," he said. "You will fall on your behind."

"Then help me."

He moved behind me and grasped my shoulders. His grip was firm, reassuring, fatherly.

"First, you need to find your balance," he said. "Your *chi,* as the Chinese say." Now he reached around and pushed his fist against my abdomen, about three inches below my navel.

"When you move around the bag—when you walk down the street, for that matter—imagine there's a train running through you right at this spot. You feel it?" He took my hand and put it over the area. "Now relax and let me move your arms and legs."

I relaxed as much as I could.

"You want to be as small a target as possible," Goodman said. "Since you're right-handed, step forward with your left foot. Stop. Good. Now shift your weight to that foot, but remember the train. That's it."

Goodman was animated, beaming. The born teacher teaching again. I wondered why he ever quit.

"Swing your left shoulder so it's lined up with your left foot. Lift your right heel. Head up. Don't look at the train, just feel it. Now look at yourself in the mirror."

When I did I stifled a laugh. I looked like a guy surprised in the middle of a bad John Wayne impersonation.

Goodman circled me.

"Move around a little, but don't move your feet. Get comfortable with the stance."

But I felt off balance and in tiny increments slid my right foot out. As soon as I got comfortable, Goodman slid it back in with his foot.

"Now put your hands up so we can show you a proper fist."

We?

He pulled my arms up, closed my fingers, and pressed my elbows against my sides. "You must be open," he said, "but still protective enough to survive."

He moved my arms about like a puppeteer, stopping when he had my left hand cocked slightly above my shoulder, about six inches from my chin, and my right hand just below my ear, almost touching my jaw.

"Tuck your chin," he said, forcing it down with his finger. He stood back to see what he had done. "You're in business, Casey, lad," he said.

I couldn't remember ever being more uncomfortable.

"This is great," I said, addressing Goodman in the mirror, my chin still tucked to my chest. "As long as I never have to move."

"That'll be next," he said, rubbing the indentation in his forehead. Then he went into the kitchen to make a cup of tea and cut up oranges for the cockatiels.

"There are metaphors everywhere," I heard him say, though I didn't know if he was talking to me.

CHAPTER 20

Gradually, the way I had for so long spent my days and nights changed. I weaned myself from the addictive late nights of beer and tobacco out by the pool. I did it simply because, if I hadn't, the next day the push-ups and sit-ups and running would make my head pound and my ears ring. I enjoyed the vigorous exercise, the way the muscles tightened and the blood rushed to my skin.

M. P. didn't know what to make of this routine, and when I'd drop to the floor to do a set or two, she'd scamper from the room with a cry of consternation.

I didn't take to this new lifestyle naturally. Not at all. The push-ups hurt my back and wrists, and the sit-ups often left me doubled in pain, my stomach muscles in knots. Each breath seared my lungs as I ran, but I found that I could push it a few blocks farther every day. Although the pipe was easy to give up, the beer was a bear to ditch. Not drinking freed up more time than I knew what to do with, but now, at least, I had something to do.

I hung out at the Conservancy and talked to a naturalist there about the owl I had seen. After hearing a description, she told me it was probably a barred owl, once very common in southwest Florida but now quite rare. I asked what it might've been doing on my porch swing at dawn, and the girl said it was probably looking for a place to roost. So I picked up some plywood at the hardware store, untangled my rusty old hand tools, and set about building a nesting box for a displaced barred owl. While I sawed and banged (bending at least a dozen nails) and painted, I spent an embarrassing amount of time crafting what I would like in a nice box home if I were an owl. Though late October, it was still plenty hot for this sort of work, but I didn't mind because now, each time I'd sweat, I'd feel just a little bit cleaner.

I began reading again. Nothing threatening just yet—collections of Calvin and Hobbes comics, mail-order catalogs, a slim volume that Goodman had given me of Byron's *Manfred and Other Poems,* and a book of birdhouse plans.

One afternoon, as I watered pagoda bushes and Gin's neglected Christmas cacti, I noticed Jason Foster sitting on the front steps next door, baseball glove in hand. When he caught my eye, I looked away, afraid of frightening him inside when it was such a beautiful day to be outdoors. Glove on, he popped the ball into the pocket again and again. When I looked again, he was gazing at me, wary but at least not spooked.

I turned off the water and went inside, flung open the doors of the hall closet and tossed out boots, umbrellas, a life jacket, and musty sweaters until I uncovered my baseball glove, unused for at least a decade. I slipped on the rug hurrying to get back outside.

Jason was still there and smiled, bashful, when I held up my glove. Then he stood, reared back, and heaved the ball far up into the Cuban laurel, shouting, "Sorry," as I stumbled over tangled roots to retrieve it.

"That's okay," I said.

I motioned us out near the street beyond the thickest branches and we threw. *Smack . . . thwok. Smack . . . thwok. Smack . . . thwok.* Soon we'd set up that beautiful rhythm of a game of catch that I hadn't known since I'd last thrown a ball with my father.

Smack . . . thwok. Receiving and delivering. Accepting and giving. And just as when I'd played with my father, Jason and I threw in silence. To have said anything would've ruined it.

I spent a lot of time thinking about Eleanora, too.

I missed her each day. Not the way I still missed Gin. I wanted Gin back for so many reasons. I missed Eleanora for the way she softened the days. Some women could do that with nothing more than their presence, no matter if they smoked, drank, cussed like seamen, or (in Eleanora's case) saved my ass on a sidewalk in Miami. And if they might not be quite flesh and blood, well, what did that matter either, really?

Then there was my mother-in-law.

I had barely had time to enjoy the last brushstroke of brown paint on my owl house when Phyllis swerved into the driveway, taking the corner too short and crushing a foot-wide swath of wandering Jew. I exhaled and pressed the lid on the paint can.

"Hi, Casey," she said, coming over to stand beside me. She dipped into the pocket of her smock and fetched out a cigarette, cupping her hands to light it. She exhaled like a locomotive.

"What are you doing?" she said, eyeing my creation.

"I'm making a birdhouse."

"Where's your friend? Eleanor, wasn't that her name?"

Phyllis and Bob had finally accepted Eleanora's existence, although they had never met her.

"She's gone away for a while."

"Oh," Phyllis said. She flicked an ash, and I watched as it drifted too close to the wet paint. "I mean, I know you're probably lonely, but she didn't seem quite right for you."

I turned away before rolling my eyes.

"I wanted to come over sooner, but Bob was afraid of bothering you. But I decided you're still family, and I came by to see how you're doing."

"I certainly appreciate that," I said. The owl house seemed to need another coat of paint in the worst way, and I popped open the can and dipped my brush.

Phyllis commented that I appeared to have lost weight. Was I sick? No, I was just getting in shape for the first time in years, I told her, being careful not to mention why I was shaping up, for fear she'd sic Dr. Gonzalez on me again.

"What you need to do is get out more," Phyllis said. She dropped her cigarette and crushed it with her toe. Right on the patio bricks. "It's what Virginia would want. You know that, don't you?"

I looked up from my painting and nodded politely, though it was not at all what Gin would want. She would want me to finish something—*finish at least one goddamn thing*—so I could put her ghost to rest and live the rest of my life in some sort of peace.

"I finished this owl house," I found myself saying aloud.

"That's wonderful," Phyllis said. "But you're not going to pay the bills by building birdhouses, and you're not going to keep your sanity, either. Bob and I think you need to go out and get some kind of a job. Any job. For your own sake."

She then leaned close and squeezed me next to her. "We worry about you," she said. "Without Virginia, we feel obligated to take care of you."

I smiled and carefully put the lid back on the paint can. I tamped it down with the handle of a screwdriver. Then I went over to a spigot on the side of the house and rinsed the brush thoroughly. I returned flicking clear water from the bristles.

"Phyllis," I said, "please don't come by anymore."

With that, an amazing thing happened. I did a double take as her cheeks sagged, her shoulders sagged, her whole body seemed to grow heavier, tugged hard by gravity, as she turned and walked to her car. I watched her open the door and lower herself in. Before she could start it, I got in on the passenger side. Phyllis's face was puffy and red.

"I'm sorry," I said. "I'm so sorry."

She looked straight ahead and nodded slightly. With the windows up, the engine silent, the car created an intimacy that was overwhelming, unavoidable. I wondered where to begin.

"Do you hate us?" she said. "I mean Bob and me. Ever since Virginia . . ." Her face grew even redder until she released it in little-girl tears, and I felt the pain I would feel watching my own mother cry. I hugged her awkwardly, over the console, around the steering wheel.

"I've hated myself," I said. "But there was too much of it for just me, I think. So I spread it around to everyone and everything. I wanted a reason to hate you after Gin died, so it wasn't hard to find one."

Phyllis turned to me, bumping the horn with her elbow, making us both jump.

"Sorry," she said. "I don't know why Bob bought a compact."

I sighed.

"I resented the way you two seemed to get on with your lives," I said. "But if you'd come apart, I would've resented that, too. Does that make any sense?"

"No," she said. "There is a lot you don't understand, Casey. Gin was my baby. My first and in a lot of ways my favorite. That's right, parents have favorites. And you have no idea—*no idea*—what it feels like to lose a baby. The only thing that kept me together was being a mother. To Bob, to the other kids, even to you, even though my daughter was gone. Once you're a mother, you can never stop."

She started to say "Does *that* make sense?" but she welled into tears again.

I gave her another clumsy hug and said, "I could use a mother, Phyllis, if you're still offering."

"Just don't call me *Mom*," she said.

CHAPTER 21

Goodman and I worked out together three days a week, moving through footwork—a sort of controlled shuffle to keep me from getting tangled in my own feet—and defensive maneuvers, such as blocking and ducking, though the big bag of sand wasn't likely to punch back.

I'd bought a stiff and cracking pair of boxing gloves from a secondhand sporting goods store, and Goodman carefully laced them for me each time I visited.

Finally, I actually started hitting the damned bag. I moved around it as Goodman had, hitting it with both hands, shifting my weight from foot to foot as I did, keeping my center level. The bag shivered and swung ferociously on its hook, and I understood Goodman's Byronic nuttiness. This was not about boxing at all, or even about getting in shape. It was about the balance that Goodman had stressed, the fusion of mind and body, with practice, into accomplishment, no matter how seemingly pointless. And there wasn't much that seemed more pointless on the surface than banging on a big bag in an old house on the beach.

It was about doing something.

★　★　★

One afternoon, over slices of Key lime pie at a café, Goodman told me how happy he was that we'd been able to hook up again after all these years. He said he had little family and few friends left alive and that he'd awakened one night some months before with the understanding that when his time came, he'd be checking out completely alone. He didn't sleep well the next few nights.

I picked at my pie and wished I could guarantee him that I or someone else would be there with him, if that was what he wanted.

"I've been wondering about something, Goodman."

His washed-out blue eyes met mine.

"How did you know where I was? I don't recall ever mentioning to you that I was moving to Naples."

"Curious thing," he said, putting a small piece of pie crust into his mouth before putting down his fork. "Shortly after Mother passed, I got a phone call from a friend of yours. She said to be sure to look you up when I got down this way. But I can't recall her name."

I didn't need her name. I knew it had been Eleanora.

With time on my hands one morning, I set to tidying up the bungalow, beginning with the guest bedroom, Eleanora's room. I pulled up the blinds for more light, stripped the sheets from Eleanora's bed, and was instantly embarrassed by the condition of the old mattress, with its missing buttons and threadbare patches. I hoisted it to flip it over, turning it perpendicular, being careful not to foul the ceiling fan or smash out a window.

Then something beneath the mattress caught my eye. A spiral-bound notebook. I let the mattress fall against the wall, sending M. P. headlong from the room, and I opened the notebook to reveal the peaks and sharp angles of a very familiar handwriting:

My dearest Casey,

It's late, and you are asleep while I am awake. Or perhaps it's you who are awake while I sleep. (Isn't that the mind game one of our philosophy profs used to play? Remember how it used to bother me?)

I'm feeling philosophical myself tonight and thought I might as well share with you, my buddy. We've both been so preoccupied lately it seems we've barely seen each other, much less touched or laughed. I miss you.

My job has been a bitch, more so than I've let on (nobody likes a whiner). Clients have been particularly difficult this season. One even asked me to pick up her dry cleaning the other day. So now I'm a gofer, too.

I never wanted to be a designer, you know. When we met and fell in love, I thought I'd be an artist, willing to suffer for years, if that's what it took, to create something. What pretentious nonsense. Pretty soon I knew that if we were to share a life, at least one of us had to be practical, at least part of the time, and I didn't know if it would be you or me. (I often think about this: What if we had not passed each other in the hallway that Friday afternoon so many years ago? What if you had bent to get a drink and I had walked behind you and we'd never seen each other again? It was a big campus, after all. Where would you and I be now, do you think?)

But we did meet, and quickly, in a very palpable way, I needed you, couldn't live without you, and I knew you felt the same about me. But what I've come to realize recently, sweetheart, is that I also needed to be needed by you. Not in a neurotic, clinging way, I hope, but so that we could help each other live a good life, no regrets at the end.

I think in a way everybody needs everybody else, and if we can recognize that and help each other out, well, I think we've gone a long way toward making sense of it all.

I just want to say that I like the novel you've been working on. More than anything, I've enjoyed that you've shared it with me in the evenings. Is it the best you can do? I hardly think so. But it could be *a step to something fine. I'm talking about your life, Casey, dear. What I want to ask you is this—Will you please go ahead and live and enjoy all the beauty and love and sorrow and aggravation that come with it? Smear it on your hands and face like blackberry juice, roll in it, offer it to someone else. Live, my dearest, don't be afraid. I am so close you can almost touch me. And you are so close to waking.*

I have memorized the smell of your neck, the hard swell of your chest, the golden hollow beneath your arm, the slant of your smile. They'll stay with me forever.

Before I turn off the light, I want to say, please don't mind Mom. She tries. I love your owl house. The silly hope behind it is simply beautiful. You will always make me smile.

I love you, pal,

Gin

Mechanically, I put the notebook back and pulled the mattress on top of it. Then I took two steps and passed out cold, my cheek pressed to the cool tile floor.

CHAPTER 22

Thanksgiving had come and gone, with Mashed Potatoes and me sharing a couple of Hungry Man turkey dinners and watching college football. Phyllis had invited me to a family gathering, but I said I'd been away from the house a lot lately and that M. P. was feeling neglected. I did appreciate her asking, though she didn't quite seem to understand about the cat.

Meanwhile, my little bungalow was going to hell, more so than usual. Ixora plants were beginning to grow through the ill-fitting awning windows, and Mr. Foster next door, owner of a nursery and landscaping business, made a special point of eye-balling my overgrown lawn whenever he'd catch me outside. It was pretty clear that I'd have to win the lottery and walk up and down the street shoveling twenties out of a wheelbarrow to win some of my neighbors back.

Every day I'd make a careful check of my owl house to see if my early-morning phantom had miraculously returned, but it was always empty save an occasional tree frog or two. So I called the Conservancy to ask how I might attract a barred owl.

The naturalist who answered the phone recognized my voice.

"Who cooks for you?" she said.

"I beg your pardon?"

"Whooo cooks for youuuu?"

"Well, I make most of my own meals," I said after a pause. "But I wouldn't exactly call it cooking. Tuna, black beans and rice . . ."

The woman laughed.

"No," she said. " 'Who cooks for you?' is the call of a barred owl. That's what it sounds like, anyway. You know, 'Whooo coooks for youuuu.' If you record that and play it near where you want the bird to nest, it may think another owl is looking for a mate."

"Who cooks for you," I repeated.

"Yes," she said. "Kind of cute, don't you think?"

I didn't have a tape recorder, so I recorded my mating call on the answering machine, stretching the cord to its limit and placing it on a chair under the vacant owl house. I had rerecorded it at least a dozen times, trying to sound as seductively owlish as possible, finally making myself laugh like a monkey.

Dusk was the best time to try it, and I sat as unobtrusively as possible beneath the Cuban laurel and punched the button repeatedly for the tape's thirty-second bursts of "Who cooks for you? Whoo coooks for youuuu?"

Potter Solewecki emerged from between the houses carrying a bin of cans and bottles to the curb. Figuring it would be worse for me to jump up and shut the machine off, I stared at him and he at me as the machine cooed and cooed, "Who cooks for you?" Old Potter shook his head. I waved. He finished his errand quickly and hustled back to his house.

"Happy holidays," I shouted to his back. He waved a hand before shutting the door.

The morning after Gin died I lay quietly and very alone in bed, nursing the worst headache of my life. I did nothing to dull the pain except pray for a respite from the relentless telephone. The sheets still smelled like Virginia, the pillows like her shampoo, and I breathed it all in until it choked me with irony and regret. With one eye closed, and pressing a palm to my temple, I stripped the beds and threw the load into the washer. I remade the bed with some old sheets from college that I found shoved way back in a closet and that were musty from disuse. I tucked the corners in tightly, the way Gin had always done, and lay back down and closed my eyes.

The phone rang once, and I sat up, waiting for another ring that didn't come. Absently, I looked down at the yellowed sheets, and my blood turned to ice water. On the bed, dancing in the breeze from the ceiling fan, was a single long brown hair of Virginia's. It squiggled and jumped erratically, like a garden snake chopped with a spade.

I flattened the strand with my hand and drew it between my fingers to its full length. I put it between the pages of a book on the nightstand, obsessively memorizing the page number, and then pulled the phone from the wall.

As one might expect, since I'd found Virginia's letter, I'd been checking under the mattress in Eleanora's room like an anxious lover checks the mail. I took to sitting on the floor next to the bed, staring at the separation between the mattresses, willing a message to arrive. The afternoon of December 24, I overturned the mattress and sucked in a breath. Atop the box spring was a card—a business card—yellow and folded. It said *The Dome, 3 Beacom Boulevard, Miami. Jazz Nightly.* On the back, in writing I didn't recognize, was *9 P.M., Dec. 24.*

At seven I filled the car with gas and headed east.

I got lost, of course, in downtown Miami, driving round and round beneath swaying holiday greetings and cheesy aluminum snowmen attached to streetlights. I found Beacom Boulevard by accident and pulled up at The Dome about half past nine. On the sidewalk I looked around. I had been down this street, I was certain, on other trips to the city. I didn't know how I hadn't seen this club before. It seemed the only place alive on a street of abandoned buildings.

A sign on the door read OPEN MIKE NITE MERRY XMAS, and I slipped in and found a tiny table along the wall, as inconspicuous as I could be, the only one in the room without a date.

I listened to the house band, a decent trio with guitar, piano, and bass, until a waitress finally found me and I ordered a beer, breaking training because it was Christmas Eve, after all. The trio finished a set, began another, and I started to wonder about the "open-mike" business. As I looked around for the waitress to bring me another, I felt a gentle hand on my shoulder and turned to face Eleanora, her eyes moist and warm, her face as smooth as polished marble, a poinsettia flower to mark the season tucked into her tightly curled hair. She smelled of perfume, alcohol, and cigarettes.

"You're looking dry, lover," she said. "Let me fix you up." She motioned to my waitress, who arrived immediately.

"Anything he wants, for the rest of the night, it's on me," she said.

I asked her to sit down. It seemed pointless to ask where she'd been or what she'd been doing, so I sat for a long moment staring at her, a silly smile on my face. I was glad to see her.

"Talk to me," I finally said. The waitress set down another beer for me and something dark and medicinal looking for Eleanora.

"Well, I know what you've been doing," she said, a throaty coyness in her voice as if I'd been up to no good. "And, sugar, you look good enough to eat."

I flushed and looked at the tabletop, glancing up in time to see Eleanora polish off her drink in one quick toss.

I took several swallows of beer, which tasted better than I had remembered, and then I blurted it out.

"You have a power over me that I just can't . . ."

We were interrupted by a man who appeared from behind me, wrapped an arm around Eleanora's shoulders, and whispered into her ear. He was playing Cool Jazz Man for all he was worth, sporting dark glasses and a purple beret, a starched white shirt open to the waist. He departed without acknowledging me.

"Who's that asshole?" I said.

Eleanora smiled and put a hand on top of mine. "I'm the entertainment," she said and stood to go.

"You're amateur night?"

Over her shoulder she said, "Yeah, ain't that some off-time jive?"

* * *

The lights dimmed and Eleanora disappeared off to the side of the stage. In the eerie red glow of a strand of Christmas bulbs hung behind the stage, the guy who had stopped at our table stepped up to the microphone, yanked it from its stand, and practically swallowed it.

"Good evening, ladies and gentlemen of the night," he murmured, the muffled words barely distinguishable. "Our featured singer tonight comes to us from I don't know where. Let's call her an early Christmas present, a gift of the Magi. And if she don't look familiar to you, if you don't think she's something real gone and great, brothers and sisters, you ain't lived right. Put it together now for The Lady." He lowered his head theatrically and gestured toward the far side of the room, where a pinprick of light soon widened to reveal the broad, beaming face, eyes liquid and alive. Accompanied by the spot, Eleanora strolled to the stage, took the mike from the man, and thanked him. He again whispered in her ear, making her giggle and me feel strangely uneasy.

She began with "Summertime," a slow, sultry version that by

song's end had the audience hooked. She had buffed off every speck of rust since I'd last heard her sing. Her voice had not a crack, not a quaver, not a waver. I was listening to Lady Day in her prime, and she was damned good. She segued into an upbeat version of "What a Little Moonlight Will Do," and instead of seeing her in the glare and smoke of the club, I pictured her back in my bedroom that first night, a night now so distant it seemed like a piece of another life. As she sang, *"You get bold/You can't resist him/And all you say/When you have kissed him . . ."* I felt an ache in my gut that I hadn't felt in a long, long time, and I had to admit to myself that at some point, I don't know when, really, I had fallen in love with her.

She sang, *"Hush now, don't explain/You're my joy and pain . . ."* and wrapped herself so completely around these words that I thought she offered me her soul to keep.

Many in the crowd nodded to the music or swayed in their seats, eyes closed. After each song the spotlight narrowed again to a dot, and the audience shouted its approval.

". . . Cold or wet, tired, you bet/All this I'll soon forget/With my man . . . with my maaaaaan . . ."

Her set lasted a good hour, though it seemed just minutes, and before she stepped from the stage, she smiled and bowed to the folks on their feet, then shot me a glance and a wink. I winked back, too late, and, very uncool, flashed her a thumbs-up sign.

Mr. Beret & Shades helped her from the stage—she hardly needed it—and, still holding her arm, ushered her to the bar where several drinks were waiting. Eleanora tossed hers back and went to light a cigarette, but her new friend stopped her hand midway and flicked a lighter of his own. He then whispered to her again—did he quickly kiss her neck?—and she laughed loud and long. And then, together, they left.

I finished my beer and after several wrong turns, bumping elbows and sloshing drinks, I found the way out to my car. Blinking away hot tears, I told myself I must've drunk too fast.

CHAPTER 23

When I finally got home and got to bed, I slept deeply for only an hour or two, then hovered just near waking for almost as long. A strange, repetitive sound wormed through my brain, a distant choking or gagging of some sort. Unusual sounds at night rarely meant anything good, so I roused myself enough to get up and investigate. First I checked Mashed Potatoes. She lay sound asleep like a little queen atop a stack of pillows on Virginia's side of the bed. Grateful it wasn't her, a got a pen light from my dresser to look around. A cursory check of the bathrooms and kitchen revealed no drips or leaks or breaks, and I stopped and flicked off the light to better concentrate on the sound. It came from everywhere and nowhere, seeping through the walls; just when I thought I'd located it, it arose in a dozen other places. Sleep now was out of the question, so I put on a robe and quietly opened the front door. A cool breeze drifted in, delightful because it was so rare. I stepped just outside the door and listened. The sound was coming from somewhere near the giant Cuban laurel tree, perhaps even from the tree itself. Fighting a sudden surge of the creeps, I walked closer and stared into the darkness of the twisted trunk pillars. Slowly, a figure separated itself from the tree and called my name.

"Eleanora?" I said, and she began to sob heavily.

"Casey," she said, "I need you."

Tripping over knobby roots, I went over to where she sat, and sat facing her.

"What is it?"

She didn't respond, only choked on tears. I put my arm around her and noticed for the first time that she was wearing a man's white shirt, and apparently that was all. I could see the swell of her breasts where she'd mismatched buttons and buttonholes.

I tilted her head toward me and studied her features. In addition to tear streaks there were streaks of blood that had run to the collar of the shirt. A large swelling on her cheek had partially closed her left eye, and the corner of her mouth was hard with crusted blood.

"Jesus."

"You should see *him.*"

"What happened?"

"I picked the wrong man. Again."

I gently stroked her face, avoiding the swollen areas, and Eleanora's eyes closed.

Impulsively, I kissed her cheek. Eyes still shut, she turned her head and pressed her mouth to mine, hard. I tasted the salt of tears and blood and licked traces of both from her lips.

What followed was like the warped reality of a dream. I can't be sure it wasn't a dream. I helped Eleanora inside, sat her on the edge of the bathtub, and with a washcloth dabbed the blood from her face. I rinsed the cloth, wrapped some ice cubes in it, and gently pressed it against the swellings on her cheek and lip. She looked back at me with wide, childlike eyes, and I remembered what she had said the first night we met: *It's amazing what a child will endure because she thinks she's supposed to.*

"You're not just Eleanora, simply Eleanora," I whispered. "Tonight at the club you were unbelievable."

She closed her eyes again as I kissed them, and when I lifted her up, she wrapped her arms around me. I took her into my bedroom—did I carry her?—and helped her into bed.

"It's late," I said, crawling in next to her.

"It's not too late," she said.

And we made love—long, slow, deep, dreamlike. I came with a comforting warmth, then fell asleep with my face pressed against her dew- and leaf-scented hair.

When I opened my eyes, I found Eleanora still beside me. It was Christmas morning.

I stayed in bed till after noon, afraid to get up, afraid that by disturbing even the air around us that I'd somehow cause Eleanora to vanish. I did not want to lose her again. So I stroked M. P.'s tangled fur and watched out the window as one by one the neighbors' yards filled with cars disgorging scores of friends and relatives carrying casserole dishes and pretty packages. I wouldn't have minded joining one of the parties for the evening. I would, of course, take Eleanora. It was Christmas, after all. We didn't need to be a part of the festivities; no one needed to scrounge up gifts for us. We could just sit back and enjoy the surprise—feigned or real—on the faces of the other guests as they opened their presents. But it was unlikely. I had ignored my neighbors, and I had turned down too many casual invitations to get together for coffee or a drink.

Instead, I turned over, pulled Eleanora's hair back from her face, and ran my tongue lightly across her neck. She opened her eyes, locked full wet lips on mine, and pulled me closer, and I felt myself tumbling again into a fever-dream mix of passion and confusion. If one can have his soul devoured, that was how I felt.

Afterward, I fell asleep again briefly but then awoke energized. Eleanora was already up, so, no longer bothering to put on shorts (there didn't seem much point), I went to find her. I had awakened with an idea.

Eleanora stood before the mirror in the room where she used to sleep, wearing my bathrobe, untied, and pulling a hairbrush slowly through thick tresses.

"Do you have plans?" I said, smiling as I imagined some ghostly Christmas blowout.

Eleanora paused, brush poised above her head, and looked at me, her eyes sinking slowly to my groin, where they lingered. Never an overly modest sort, I nevertheless felt my abdomen tighten and my neck flush.

"Baby doll," she said, "today I am yours."

We looked at each other, silent, for a long moment, and I finally said, "Then let's get dressed. There's someone I'd like you to meet."

CHAPTER 24

When we arrived at Goodman Hardin's back door, Eleanora looking especially stunning in her navy blue, I dangled a fifth of Jim Beam between thumb and forefinger. It'd be enough for Eleanora, with a couple of drinks for me, and Goodman no longer drank.

I knocked, heard him holler, "I've been expecting you. Come in," and pulled open the screen door, allowing Eleanora to enter first. We walked the gauntlet of birds without a shriek, not even a peep.

Goodman met us in the gathering room, hugged me, and wished me a merry Christmas. I returned the greeting and turned and gestured toward Eleanora.

"Goodman, um, I'd like you to meet . . ."

But introductions, it seemed, weren't necessary. Goodman looked at Eleanora, his eyes wide with recognition and, for a moment, I thought, fear.

But the Southern gentleman quickly recovered and took Eleanora's hand and kissed it.

"Many thanks," he said, "for brightening an old man's holiday."

"How charming," Eleanora said, and curtsied with exaggerated coyness.

The next thing I knew, Goodman had pressed his wallet in my hand and said, "Two bottles of aquavit, if you would be so kind, sir, and whatever else you and the lady would like. This should be a celebration."

"Are you sure?" I said, thinking of his doctor's advice.

Goodman nodded.

"Don't be long, lover," Eleanora called as I closed the screen door.

★   ★   ★

A rare winter storm was grinding its way through the northeastern Gulf headed south, and onshore breezes had already developed a bite by the time I got back to the beach house. The fronds of coconut palms rattled and groaned in the wind. Pines showered needles, and I hunched my shoulders to try to keep warm. In the fading light, the beach was an unusually forlorn place, and whipping sand felt like tiny stinging insects on my skin.

But Goodman's place was jumping. Scratchy music blared discordantly from speakers too small to handle the volume. On the porch, cockatiels bobbed on their perches, and for an instant I thought they were keeping time with the music. Instead, no doubt, they were just staying warm.

"I've missed you, lover," Eleanora said above the music as I set the sack of clinking bottles on the table next to the half-empty bottle of Jim Beam. She and Goodman sat like kids on the floor of the gathering room, next to a leather record hassock, 78s spread around them.

"Come and make your selections," Goodman said, looking up and smiling. I could tell by the gleam in his eyes that he'd already joined Eleanora for drinks.

I felt welcome and warm and happy, and I poured myself a long glass of aquavit, the comforting aroma of caraway conjuring images of holiday pastries and Midwestern kitchens. I went over and joined the party.

★   ★   ★

"Why didn't you tell me about this extraordinary woman?" Goodman whispered to me.

"I'll try to someday," I said. I was getting drunk quickly on the unusual liquor.

Goodman shook his head, looked beyond me. "Remarkable. Simply remarkable."

"Dance with me, sugar," Eleanora said, startling us both.

"Would you do the honors?" Goodman said to me, pointing at the stack of records.

With few exceptions, I didn't know what I was looking at, so I chose songs by the appeal of their titles. I put on "Key Largo" by Anita O'Day, and Goodman and Eleanora danced slowly around the room, their figures mirrored on every wall. Then I dropped on "Lonely Street," by someone named Charlie Barnett, and then Herb Jeffries's "Flamingo," two more slow tunes.

"Pick it up a little, Casey, before this old man falls asleep," Goodman said. He smiled at me and winked.

"Give me a hint," I said.

He came over, quickly flipped through the stacks, slipped a few on the turntable, and he and Eleanora really began to boogie.

"Slide Hamp Slide"—and Goodman flipped Eleanora about like a stuffed toy. She squealed with delight. On "Cuba" Eleanora switched roles and had Goodman spinning till I thought he'd lose more pieces. She lifted him from the floor, sidling him on each hip before putting him down.

I swallowed aquavit and watched. Between sets, Goodman, laughing and panting, drank directly from the bottle, palming one empty at the fireplace where it crashed against the stone.

"Casey," he said, before returning to the dance floor, "I have always understood the appeal of that."

They did not lose a step. To "The House of Blue Lights" Eleanora mouthed the words as she jabbed Goodman in the chest with her finger:

"*What's that, homey? If you think I'm going dancin' on a dime, your clock is clickin' on the wrong time!*"

Goodman picked up his part, mouthing, "*Well what's your pleasure, treasure? You call the plays, I'll dig the ways. You snap the whip, I'll make the trip . . .*"

It was ridiculous and delightful and they danced and danced and I laughed so hard I had trouble seeing and I remember Goodman quoting Byron *(Though the night was made for loving/And the day returns too soon, /Yet we'll go no more a roving/By the light of the moon.)* and I drank more and more and soon I couldn't see at all until I woke up at home in bed with no idea how I got there.

By then, Eleanora was gone and Goodman Hardin was dead.

CHAPTER 25

A neighbor had been the last to see him. She'd heard music—uncharacteristically loud—from next door and had peeped out to see Goodman dancing, spinning, circling with a "colored" lady in the backyard. Though the night was cloudy and dark, she saw them as they moved back and forth through the rectangle of light from the open door, their clothes and the woman's hair snapping like laundry in the wind.

At daybreak the neighbor had gone out to the beach to poke through shells that the storm had tossed up, and she saw Goodman far out in the choppy waves. It seemed, she said, that he would anticipate a big one, then ride it in to shore on his belly.

He was bodysurfing.

Act your age, she remembered thinking.

When she next looked up, after collecting an especially polished bunch of coquina shells, Goodman had disappeared.

There were things to be done, "ducks to be put in the pond," as an old coach of mine used to say. I talked to a handler at Jungle Larry's, and she agreed to send someone out to pick up the dozen or so cranky cockatiels and find them homes. One could only guess how angry they were now.

Goodman had no living competent relatives but had told an attorney in Tallahassee that he wanted "to be cremated wherever it was convenient," his ashes scattered "anyplace they wouldn't muck things up." So I waited for a strong offshore breeze and then tossed them into it. While pressing down the pages, I read from Byron. These lines seemed appropriate—corny and grand, the way Goodman liked his verse:

> *For the sword outwears its sheath*
> *And the soul wears out the breast,*
> *And the heart must pause to breathe,*
> *And the soul itself have rest.*

"I'll see you around, ol' pal," I said, clapping the book shut.

*   *   *

This time Eleanora would not be back; I knew it in my bones. But I could not know it all. There were still some crucial pieces missing, some elements to the whole strange story I just couldn't comprehend, hard as I tried. Maybe someday I'd find the answers elsewhere.

This much was stone sure: Everyone I loved or had ever loved was gone, and I had finally worked up the nerve to join them. I was ready, and Eleanora, dear Eleanora, would escort me.

But first, I had one more thing to take care of.

*   *   *

Phyllis answered on the first ring.

"I was wondering if I might be able to stop by this evening," I said. "There's something I'd like to discuss with you."

She invited me for dinner.

Sure, she was often shrill and overbearing. And she smoked like a greasy grill. But she never let you leave her house hungry.

Bob greeted me at the door. Because it was winter, he now wore a shirt over his swim trunks. He told me I looked like I'd lost weight and led me to the dining room table where Phyllis sat, halfway through a Parliament Long and reading a paperback. She put down the book and stubbed out the butt.

"I need to check the steaks," Bob said.

I wanted to take care of matters right away, so after taking a seat I said to Phyllis, "I'll probably be going away soon, and I wondered if you might stop in and feed Mashed Potatoes. Maybe give her a little loving, too, if she comes out from under the bed."

"Oh, do you have a job interview?" she said. She hadn't completely lost her focus. Or her edge.

"Not exactly," I said. "It's something I've been working toward for a while now. But I'd rather not say what it is. I might jinx it."

"Oh." She was clearly disappointed at having a secret kept from her. Finally, she said, "Casey, I'll feed your cat. That's not a problem. But when will you be back?"

"I'm not sure. I could be gone for several days. Or longer. Could you still take care of M. P.? There's no one I'd trust more."

She frowned at the deepening mystery.

"Yes, I guess I could."

"For as long as I'm away?" I pressed.

"Casey, what's going on?" she said. "Are you in some kind of trouble? Bob, Casey's in some kind of trouble."

Bob came in carrying a plate piled high with charred meat, its origin uncertain. I went through the whole thing again with him.

"There's no trouble, I swear," I said. I reached over and placed my hand on Phyllis's. "I promise I'll tell you all about it when I get back."

I left their house stuffed and a little queasy.

When I got home I flung the mattress from Eleanora's bed and found the message I'd been waiting for. It was a brochure for the Biltmore Hotel in Coral Gables. I'd seen the pamphlet before but not for a while. Not since Gin had picked it up on our honeymoon.

Nice touch, Eleanora, I thought.

At the top was scrawled *Dec. 31, Room 304.* That was the next day, and of course I would go.

CHAPTER 26

When Gin and I were first married, I was clueless. Suddenly, I did not know how to behave. I knew how to be a date, a boyfriend, a lover, but how was a husband supposed to act? Surely not like a boyfriend, and not like a brother, and, God forbid, not like a child. My floundering began immediately—just after the ceremony. My single friends wanted to drink with me, my mother and father wanted to talk with me, and my new wife—*wife*, how odd that sounded—where the hell was she? I found her schmoozing with an old boyfriend in the corner, the one who had sent her flowers "anonymously" just that morning.

As I stood watching, a creeping feeling in my gut, a wedding guest I'd never met leaned toward me and said in my ear, "She's got you hooked, but it doesn't mean she's not still looking."

I seethed, like I figured I was supposed to. The rest of the evening, as we moved from reception to party to lounge after lounge, our entourage dwindling with each new stop, I drank too much and made a mental note of every dance Gin danced with someone else.

By the time we got home, it was ugly. I demanded to know all about the relationships she had had while we lived apart, at the same time saying my own were none of her damned business. I wanted to know why, the minute after the ceremony, she treated me like the least important person in her life. She claimed bewilderment at my behavior and slammed doors. Pictures rattled and fell from walls. Finally, all the fear and confusion and anger draining me, I fell asleep on the living room floor.

The next morning, with a pounding between my ears and a serious mad still on, I poured a cup of coffee and went out to sit by the lake behind our rented condo. Sometime later I heard footsteps in the grass, and Gin sat down next to me.

"What are we going to do?" she said, in a voice that sounded like crystal breaking. I shrugged and watched the sun dance on the water's surface. She lightly touched my shoulder with her fingers, and I turned to face her. In her eyes was the startlingly obvious. Though we'd known each other forever, it was still so early in this *new* game, and she was just as lost as I was.

I lay back in the grass and shielded my eyes from the brightness.

"Let's pretend we just got married last night," I said. "And this is the first official minute of the honeymoon."

"Sounds good to me," she said.

Left alone, the questions eventually answered themselves.

CHAPTER 27

I packed a small duffel bag, though I didn't know why. Then flat on the floor, flashlight in hand, I found M. P.'s luminous eyes beneath the bed.

"So long, fuzzball," I said.

With a groan she stretched and pulled herself out, finding easy clawholds in the already shredded underside of the mattress. She circled my feet, rubbing her scent glands on my ankles, and I picked her up, closing my eyes to better feel the vibration of her purrs. She leaped from my arms when she'd had enough.

I closed and locked the front door to the bungalow, trapping all those memories inside.

On the way to the car I spotted Jason Foster standing in his front yard. He lifted a ball and glove in a wordless request for a game of catch. And I hated to turn him down.

"Can I take a raincheck?" I said.

He nodded.

"You know, you're really a very good ballplayer," I said.

When I put the car in reverse, I had to jam the brakes to keep from running over old Potter Solewecki. My neighbors were coming out of the woodwork. He waved to me and listed to the window on his warped legs. I got out.

"Would it help to put a dead mouse in that owl cabin?" he said. "Say the word and I'll get you one."

I smiled, taken aback.

"You know, it just might," I said. "It certainly couldn't do any harm. Thanks. By the way, you know Jason Foster next door? He probably wouldn't mind lending a hand."

Potter nodded and turned to wobble between our two houses toward his backyard and wherever he kept the dead mice. I looked until he disappeared.

And I paused for a moment, watching the thinnest branches of the Cuban laurel twist and dance in the late-afternoon breeze off the Gulf. Blackbirds picked through the mat of fallen leaves while squirrels traced helixes around the trunk in a mad game of tag. M. P. sat exquisitely framed in the bedroom window. I took a deep breath and exhaled slowly, my eyes closing involuntarily. I didn't need a case of wistfulness, not now. But, damn, even a fool would've noticed that it was a beautiful afternoon.

CHAPTER 28

The overdone Moorish design of the Biltmore's lobby—the high arches, ornate columns, red velvet sofas and chairs—contrasted grossly with the simple quiet of the cool early evening outside. It had been seven years—seven years to the day, I suddenly realized—since I'd last been there, since friends had passed a hat at the reception and bought us a couple of nights as an impromptu wedding gift.

So before I went up to see what awaited in room 304, I walked around to try to remember.

In the cobblestone courtyard, wait staff bustled, getting ready for dinner. I found the table where Gin and I had dined, in an archway near the fountain, and I slid my fingertips along the linen tablecloth. I looked across at where Gin had sat, and I reached to take her hand as a busboy tipped a tray of glasses.

Had they not hit the floor, had they not smashed out a startling alarm, I never would have looked up. I never would have seen Virginia standing next to the fountain, looking at me, head tipped as if in inquiry.

I made for her as fast as I could, dodging employees, slipping on broken glass, and moving around tables and potted plants. But she moved quickly along a passageway and behind columns, disappearing around the corner without looking back.

I vaulted stairs to the third floor, went into the hallway, found room 304, and threw open the door.

"Gin?"

"No thanks, honey, I'm set," Eleanora said, scrambling ice cubes in a cocktail glass. She sat at a small table, her back to the window. On the table was a tray, and on the tray a bottle, an ice bucket, and another glass. A pack of Pall Malls sat near her left hand, and the room smelled of smoke and flowers.

"But you're looking a little dry," she said. "Would you care to join me?"

"I saw Virginia," I said.

"Fancy that," she said, and smiled in that heartbreaking way she had. "Once again, will you join me? I'll only keep asking all night."

I paused for a moment, then smiled back, slowly.

"Absolutely," I said. There was no hurry now, after all, and a few drinks could only make this easier. Besides, I wanted to talk.

I dug through my bag and pulled out the pipe and accoutrements I'd packed habitually for years. I pulled out a chair across from Eleanora and sat down. Deliberately, I righted the glass, dropped in three cubes, and filled it halfway with the astringent liquor, to which I added as much tonic water. Even the smallest movement had seemed to take on special significance, and I wondered if this were what it meant to say good-bye. I took a long, cool swallow.

"So," I said, "how've you been?"

Eleanora laughed and I laughed, and suddenly she stopped and I said, "What is it like? Death?"

She frowned and, with her fingernail, poked at a stray ash on the table.

"I don't know that I can rightly answer that, lover," she said. "Can you be more specific?"

The words wouldn't come easily, but it was something I had to know—and not for myself.

"Does it hurt? I mean, was Gin—were you—in pain?"

There was a long silence, and I stared at her big brown eyes until the rest of her face lost focus.

"Not like you think," she said at last. "Can I ask *you* something?"

"Anything."

She took a drink, finishing what was in her glass.

"What does that cute little plaque on the door mean?"

"What? What plaque?"

"Out there," she said, pointing to the door of the room. "It looks like this . . ."

And with that she pulled a pipe cleaner and another from their paper sleeve, took a cigarette from her pack, made a circle with one of the cleaners and laid it atop the cigarette, then laid the other cleaner, still straight, across them both.

I laughed. It was all too ridiculous, just too damned absurd. I laughed till tears came and the room and everything outside the window swam.

"It's a NO SMOKING sign," I finally said. "It means they don't want us to smoke in here."

To clear the air I got up and went to the window, flipping the latch and jiggling and pounding to break the ancient paint seal. When I turned back to the table to take one more look at Eleanora's goofy handiwork, I saw that it had changed. I put my hands on the table to prop myself as I looked at a pipe-cleaner heart with a pipe-cleaner arrow through it. Then I looked up and into Virginia's green eyes.

I reached to cup her face in my hands, hold her to my chest, whirl her around the room, fall with her onto the bed, and devour her. She put up her hand to stop me.

"Not yet, honey," she said, her eyes soft, full of compassion.

"What do you mean, *not yet?*"

"You're not finished."

With each step I took toward her, she stepped back. Finally I stopped, bewildered. She smiled.

"You have so much," she said, shaking her head.

"I don't have you."

She laughed. "Like it or not, you always have me."

"Gin," I said, my eyes brimming instantly, "I am so sorry."

"I'm sorry too, Case, for everything you've been through."

I reached for her again, and again she stopped me.

"There is too much left for you to do," she said. "You have to make up for both of us, you know." Her smile was steady, frustratingly reassuring.

"Come with me," I said. "We'll do it together. It'll be a little odd, maybe, but Lord knows I'm used to that by now. Just don't leave again. Please, Gin."

"Oh, my love, I wish I could explain better. You'll understand, I promise."

"I love you," she said.

This time I would not be stopped. I clutched her shoulders, leaned to kiss her, to smell her. I closed my eyes, and her lips touched mine, growing fuller, rounder, sticky like candy as they did. I opened my eyes to see Eleanora looking back at me.

"What the hell?" I said. I slammed my palm on the table, bouncing the tray, glasses, bottle, ashtray.

"Nice to see you, too, lover," Eleanora said.

"It's not fair," I said. "You give her to me for a second and then snatch her away again? Why are you doing this?"

I glanced at the table and grabbed the gin bottle.

"Look, I don't need your permission," I said. "I can break this bottle and rake it across my throat, and there isn't a damned thing anybody can do about it."

Eleanora watched me, watched my rant, with what seemed to be mild amusement, as if she were watching a child.

"But you won't," she said, "and I think you know that." She

motioned toward the chairs. "Let's sit down; I'm tired. You make me tired, lover."

I sat down reluctantly, my breath short, pulse thudding, and Eleanora again sat across from me. She looked very old now, worn out.

"I could have held her . . .," I said, pleading.

"Then you never would have let her go," Eleanora said. She sighed and closed her eyes.

"You asked if it hurt. Nope, sugar, dying doesn't hurt. But the memories'll kill you." She chuckled at her joke, eyes still shut. Then she opened them and leaned toward me, almost, but not quite, touching her hands to mine, and suddenly we seemed suspended in that room. I felt pressed to the chair. If I could've gotten up, I was certain that I'd open the door to find nothing outside of it. Not emptiness, just nothing, as if this moment were the only thing happening anywhere.

"Casey, lover," she said, "what hurts forever is what you don't do."

The thought brought me to my feet.

"That's why you're here, isn't it?"

"Natch," Eleanora said, deadpan. "I've got some atoning to do myself, child."

Now she grasped my hands, her touch light but firm, her eyes liquid and awake, her voice barely above a whisper.

"And you did that for me, lover."

I searched her face for more.

"Virginia," I said. "Is she happy?"

"Oh, yes."

She gave my hands a squeeze.

"Baby, make time," she said. "Don't be scared. Don't waste a single blessed moment."

And I knew that she was right, that Virginia had been right. I realized I'd known it for a while. It was knowledge that had arrived softly and intermittently, like the cardinals and jays in the Cuban laurel in the winter or a baseball, thrown by my shy neighbor, in the webbing of my glove or the fingertips of Goodman Hardin on my forearms as he taught me how to balance. Yet I knew it nonetheless. The understanding had slipped in quietly in the darkness with Eleanora.

Yes, I would be sticking around for a while. There was too much left to do.

★   ★   ★

The world was once again with us, alive all around us. I could see behind Eleanora to palm trees illuminated on the dark lawn and streets dotted with headlights. There would undoubtedly be a big New Year's Eve party tonight, and suddenly I was starving.

I asked Eleanora if she would please join me for dinner, Big Macs not on the menu, and she said she'd be delighted. So I took her hand and we went down to the courtyard café.

We were late for dinner, arriving past ten-thirty, but the kitchen and wait staffs were hanging around for their own party, and I persuaded them to serve us. I couldn't recall ever being so hungry. When the plates were put before us, I let the smells rise and mix and mingle and tempt: the grilled salmon crusted with pepper and lemon and ringed with slices of mango and avocado, steamed broccoli still firm to the bite, potatoes lightly whipped with garlic and butter.

It was food like I'd never tasted before, and I let each bite rest on my tongue before chewing, the flavors settling out to distinguish themselves.

And then I noticed that Eleanora had not taken a bite.

"Is your meal not good?" I said, finally putting down my fork.

"It's just fine, doll," she said softly.

"Then would you care to dance?" I said.

The band upstairs had begun its first set with "Stardust," and Eleanora and I, hand in hand, walked to the center of the patio, next to the fountain, and held each other, swaying to the music.

I had to laugh, it was all so crazy.

We danced through "I Wonder Who's Kissing Her Now," "What'll I Do?" and "Lazy Moon." Then I asked Eleanora if she would sit with me on the edge of the fountain. We sat quietly for a long time, just listening to the music, and then I said the obvious.

"You're going away, aren't you? For good this time."

She leaned and kissed my cheek.

"And that's as far as *that* goes tonight, lover," she said, smiling seductively.

I wanted to squeeze her, beg her not to go.

"Truth is, I can't touch you anymore," she said. "And you can't touch me."

I shook my head and shrugged at the silly notion.

"Too late," I said. "That's for always."

Eleanora then stood, closed her eyes, rolled her head back and, with palms upraised, sang, *"Ooohh oohh oh, what a little moonlight will doooo . . ."*

She kept on singing as she walked around the fountain, past clusters of bougainvillea and oleander, and disappeared in the darkness.

"I love you, Gin," I called.

From the ballroom above came the shouting of people anticipating the new year.

Epilogue

I returned to Naples on New Year's Day, and Mashed Potatoes greeted me at the door in her customary fashion—caterwauling for eats. So my first official domestic act of the new year was popping a can of turkey and giblets, her favorite.

There would be many more home chores to come. The place was a mess and would need considerable cleanup and repair if I were to sell it. For a long time a comfortable cocoon when I most needed it, the old bungalow had ultimately become more of a web, trapping me and all my debris in a tattered, sticky mess.

There was much I'd miss about the place, of course, like the big old Cuban laurel and, especially, its new resident. Yep, I'd succeeded in luring that homeless barred owl, or *some* barred owl, with my endless repetition of "Who cooks for you?" In Taoist fashion, she'd settled not in my carefully crafted owl house but in a tree cavity nearby. I found her one Sunday morning while I searched for Jason Foster's errant throw. As I peered into the hole, two big brown eyes popped up to meet mine. I damned near fell backward out of the tree and decided to name the bird Eleanora. That I hadn't scared her off meant she was sitting on a couple of eggs, and I wouldn't move away until I'd seen the fledglings fly.

I also got a job, though so far it's just part time. I'm director of the Goodman-Byron Foundation. It's a private program, spelled out in Goodman's will, to teach basic English, one-on-one, to Haitian and Hispanic children and adults. With the help of Goodman's attorney and others, we turned the old beach house into a school of sorts, tearing down the mirrors in the gathering room and lining the walls with books. I am also one of the tutors, and I like the job very much.

I often wonder, too, as I look at a little head bowed over a book, finger tracing the words, if I watched this child struggle ashore to a new—though not yet legal—life that dark summer night on the beach. Such a nice symmetry that would be.

At night there's still time for Billie Holiday CDs and games with M. P. and memories of Virginia. Yeah, I will always make time for that jazz.

© Jeannie Hautmann

Chad Hautmann is a former English teacher
and freelance writer whose work has appeared in
a number of literary and commercial magazines.
He lives in Naples, Florida, with his wife and two
children. This is his first novel.